A Hole in the Language

The Iowa Short Fiction Award

Prize money for the award is provided by

a grant from the Iowa Arts Council

A Hole in the Language

MARLY SWICK

UNIVERSITY OF IOWA PRESS

IOWA CITY

University of Iowa Press, Iowa City 52242
Printed in the United States of America
First edition, 1990

Some of these stories have previously appeared, in a slightly altered form, in the
North American Review, *Iowa Review*, *Playgirl*, *New Stories from the South*,
Gettysburg Review, and *California Quarterly*.

The University of Iowa Press acknowledges the generous assistance of the Kaplen
Foundation and the many private donors who helped make the publication of
this book possible. The author would like to thank the following for their
encouragement and support: the James Michener Award, University of Wisconsin
Institute of Creative Writing, National Endowment for the Arts, Breadloaf
Writers' Conference, MacDowell Colony, Helene Wurlitzer Foundation, and Barney
Karpfinger.

Printed on acid-free paper

Library of Congress Cataloging-in-Publication Data
Swick, Marly A., 1949–
A hole in the language/Marly Swick.—1st ed.
p.   cm.—(The Iowa short fiction award)
ISBN 0-87745-296-2 (alk. paper)
I. Title.   II. Series.
PS3569.W67   1990   90-37143
813'.54—dc20   CIP

To Shore Brenner Lipsher, *in memoriam*,

and to my parents

Contents

Elba

Mother, who wanted to keep her, always thought of her as some wild little bird—a sparrow, let loose in the wide world, lost forever—but I knew she was a homing pigeon. I knew that at some point in her flight path, sooner or later, she would make a U-turn. A sort of human boomerang. So even though I had long since stopped expecting it, I was not surprised when I walked down the gravel drive to the mailbox, which I'd painted papaya yellow to attract good news, and found the flimsy envelope with the Dallas postmark. I didn't know a soul in Dallas, or Texas for that matter, but the handwriting reminded me of someone's. My own.

I walked back inside the house and hung my poncho on the peg by the door.

"Still raining?" Mother asked. She was sitting in her new electric wheelchair in front of the TV, painting her fingernails a neon violet. Mother's sense of color was pure aggression. This was one of her good days. On the bad days, her hands trembled so that she could barely hold a spoon, let alone that tiny paintbrush.

"Just let up," I said. "Sun's poking through." I handed her the new *People* magazine, which she insisted upon subscribing to. "You know anyone in Dallas, Mother?"

"Not so as I recall." She dabbed at her pinky with a cotton-ball. Mother was vain about her hands. I was used to how she looked now, but I noticed people staring in the doctor's waiting room. She had lost some weight and most of her hair to chemotherapy, and I guess people were startled to see these dragon-lady nails on a woman who looked as if she should be lying in satin with some flowers on her chest.

"Why do you ask?" she said.

I opened the envelope and a picture fluttered into my lap. It was a Polaroid of a sweet-faced blond holding a newborn baby in a blue blanket. Their names and ages were printed neatly on the back. Before I even read the letter I knew. I knew how those Nazis feel when suddenly, after twenty or thirty un-

3

eventful years, they are arrested walking down some sunny street in Buenos Aires. It's the shock of being found after waiting so long.

"What's that?" Mother said.

I wheeled her around to face me and handed her the Polaroid. She studied it for a minute and then looked up, speechless for once, waiting for me to set the tone.

"That's her," I said. "Her name's Linda Rose Caswell."

"Lin-da Rose." She pronounced it phonetically, as if it were some foreign gibberish.

I nodded. We looked at the picture again. The blond woman was seated on a flowered couch, her wavy hair just grazing the edge of a dime-a-dozen seascape in a cheap gilt frame. I hoped it was someone else's living room, some place she was just visiting.

Mother pointed to the envelope. "What's she say?"

I unfolded the letter, a single page neatly written.

"She says she's had my name and address for some time but wanted to wait to contact me until after the birth. The baby's name is Blake and he weighs eight pounds, eight ounces, and was born by cesarean. She says they are waiting and hoping to hear back from me soon."

"That's it?"

I nodded and handed her the letter. It was short and businesslike, but I could see the ghosts of all the long letters she must have written and crumpled into the wastebasket.

"I guess that makes you a great-grandmother," I said.

"What about you?" she snorted, pointing a Jungle Orchid fingernail at me. "You're a grandmother."

We shook our heads in disbelief. I sat silently, listening to my brain catch up with my history. Forty years old and I felt as if I had just shaken hands with Death. I suppose it's difficult for any woman to accept that she's a grandmother, but in the normal order of things, you have ample time to adjust to the idea. You don't get a snapshot in the mail one day from a baby girl you gave up twenty-four years ago saying, "Congratulations, you're a grandma!"

"It's not fair," I said. "I don't even feel like a *mother.*"

"Well, here's the living proof." Mother tapped her nail against the glossy picture. "She looks just like you. Only her nose is more aristocratic."

"I'm going to work." My knees cracked when I stood up. "You be all right here?"

Mother nodded, scrutinizing the picture in her lap. "Actually, truth to tell, I think she looks like me." She held the Polaroid up next to her face. "She's got my profile."

I felt the pleasant warmth of the sun on my shoulder blades as I walked along the path paved with sodden bougainvillea blossoms to the garage I'd had converted into a studio a few years back. I'd moved my painting paraphernalia out of the house and repapered the spare bedroom. Mother sewed some bright curtains and matching pillows for the daybed. Then we were ready for guests, and I guess we enjoyed this illusion of sociability, even though the only person who ever visited us— my mother's sister—was already dead by the time we readied the guest room.

I spent hours in the studio every day, painting still lifes, and they were hours of perfect contentment. From my studio, I could hear the ocean across the highway, but couldn't see it. Sometimes when I was absorbed in my painting, in this trance of light and color, it seemed as if my brushstrokes and the rustle of the waves were one and the same.

After Mother and I moved to Florida, I developed a passion for citrus fruits. I liked to look at them, and I was always fondling them. When I was pregnant, the only food I could tolerate was oranges. I lived on oranges. One afternoon while I was wandering around Woolworth's, wasting time before returning to the motel, I bought a tin of watercolors just on impulse. That afternoon I sat down at the Formica table in our kitchenette at the motel and painted a picture of a red china dish with one lemon in it. As soon as the paint was dry, Mother said, "My, I never knew you had such an artistic bent," and taped it to the dwarf refrigerator. Even with my big belly, I felt like a proud first-grader. From then on, hardly a day's gone by that I haven't painted something.

My father back home in Baltimore made it clear he wasn't awaiting our return. Seduced by sunshine, we decided to stay in Florida after the baby was born. We moved out of the motel into a rented house on Siesta Key, and Mother enrolled me in an adult art class. The teacher, an excitable Cuban, nudged me to enter some local art shows. Now galleries as nearby as Miami and as far away as Atlanta sell my work on a regular basis. A local newspaper reporter interviewed me a few years back and quoted me as saying, "Painting is meditation on the moment, no past and no future." Mother sent my father a copy of the article, which he never acknowledged, although he continued to send us monthly checks, like clockwork, until the divorce settlement. I thought maybe the quote offended him.

The evening of the day we received the Polaroid, after the supper dishes were cleared, I spent a good long time in front of the medicine chest mirror. I felt as if I were saying good-bye to someone. Then I climbed up on the toilet seat and from there onto the rim of the sink. Using a washcloth as a pot holder, I unscrewed the light bulb. It was one of those guaranteed-to-outlast-you 100-watters.

I carried the offending bulb into the living room. Mother was hunched underneath the pole lamp browsing through some old black-and-white snapshots, the kind with the wavy edges.

"Just hold on a sec," I said, as I unplugged the lamp and fumbled to exchange light bulbs.

"What're you doing?" Mother said. "It was just fine the way it was."

Mother always got nervous when I tried to change anything around the place. She would have appreciated living at the scene of a murder, sealed off by the police, with no one allowed to touch a thing.

"I'm putting in a brighter bulb," I said. "You're going to ruin your eyes."

"That's too glary." She squinted up at me as soon as I plugged the lamp back in.

"It's much better." I slipped the 60-watt bulb into my pocket.

In the bright light I recognized the pictures she was looking at, and even after all that time, my stomach muscles clutched. They were snapshots we had taken on the drive down here to Florida from Maryland almost twenty-five years ago. I had a new instamatic camera my father had given me for my birthday, before he found out, and I couldn't resist using it, even though I knew that I would never want to look at those pictures.

"Look at that." I picked up a picture of Mother holding a basket of nuts at a pecan stand in Georgia. She was wearing a patterned sundress with spaghetti straps, and she had a bird's nest of blond hair. "Imagine," I said. "You were younger there than I am now."

I handed the picture back to her and squeezed her bony shoulder. She reached up and patted my hand. It was hard to guess who felt worse.

I picked up another snapshot—Mother in her bathing cap with the rubber petals that resembled an artichoke, posed like Esther Williams in the shallow end of a swimming pool.

"I'd forgotten that bathing cap," I laughed.

"I'd forgotten that body," she sighed.

Some of the motels had small pools. Looking at the picture, I could smell the chlorine. At night, under the artificial lights, the water turned a sickly jade green. It was summer, and after a hot, sticky day in the car, nothing looked more inviting than those little concrete pools surrounded by barbed wire, but I was embarrassed to be seen in my bathing suit with my swollen breasts and swelling belly. I would post Mother in a lawn chair. Sweating, chain-smoking, she would dutifully keep watch in the steamy night. If anyone headed toward the pool, she would whisper, "Pssst! Someone's coming!" and I would scramble up the chrome ladder into my terry-cloth beach robe. But more often than not, we would have the pool area to ourselves. Sometimes after I was through in the water, she would breaststroke a couple of slow, tired-looking laps before following me back into our room with its twin, chenille-covered beds.

Mother leafed through the little packet of snapshots as if she were looking for some particular picture. There were more shots of her—smiling beside the Welcome to Florida sign, clapping her sandals together in the surf, lugging a suitcase up the steps of an unprepossessing motel called the Last Resort. I was struck by how tired and young and lost she looked in those pictures. In my memory of those days she was strong and old and bossy. You could see in the pictures just how much it cost a woman like her to up and leave her husband, even if he was an inflexible, unforgiving, steel-reinforced ramrod of a man. The irony was that right up until he stopped speaking to me, and for a long time after, I loved him more than I loved her. I had always been a daddy's girl. I still dream of him occasionally, and in my dreams he always treats me tenderly.

"There!" Mother suddenly held a snapshot up to the light—triumphant. "There you are!"

There I was. Sitting behind the wheel of our '57 Buick (which we just sold ten years ago, all rusted from the salt air but still running), my telltale belly discreetly concealed by the dashboard. Trick photography. I seemed to be scowling at the gas pump. I was moody and sullen during the entire drive south. She did what she could to cheer me up—bought me fashion magazines and let me play the radio full blast. I had turned sixteen but didn't have my license yet. At night, even though all she wanted was a hot shower and a soft bed, she would give me driving lessons in the parking lots of the motels we stopped at. She would smile encouragingly while I stripped the gears and lurched in circles, barely missing the few parked cars with roof racks and out-of-state plates. She rarely mentioned my father, who had promised to teach me how to drive before he disowned me, but once I sauntered out of the ladies' room and caught her crying in a pay-phone booth at a gas station just across the Florida state line. Her tears relaxed something in me, just long enough for me to put an arm around her and say, "I'm sorry. I know it's all my fault."

"No," she hugged me and petted my hair. "It's his fault. He loved you too much. He thought you were perfect."

I jerked away. "I don't want to talk about him," I said. "Ever."

The whole time Mother and I were packing up the Buick, my father was in the backyard pruning the azalea bushes. I heard the angry little snips, like a dog snapping at my heels, as I trudged up and down the stairs with armloads of books and clothes. When the car was all packed, Mother and I sat in the driveway, warming the engine. We sat there waiting for him to stop us. Finally, Mother cleared her throat. "Well," she forced a brave smile. "I guess we're off."

I opened the car door and ran to the backyard. I threw my arms around my father's bent waist as he stooped over an unruly azalea. "I don't want to go!" I cried. "Don't make me go."

He shook me off and went on snipping.

"Don't you even love me?" I wailed and stomped the ground like a five-year-old.

"Look at you." He pointed the pruning shears. "Who could love that?" Then he grabbed a handful of the oversized man's shirt I was wearing and sheared a big, ragged hole that exposed my pale balloon belly.

I turned and ran back to the car.

Mother shuffled the pictures into a neat stack, like a deck of playing cards, to put away. She used to be a dedicated bridge player. After we moved, she tried to teach me a couple of times, but I have no head for card games, and anyway, you need more than two players.

"Wait a minute," I said. "What's that one there?" I pointed to an oversized picture on the bottom of the stack.

"I don't know if I ever showed you this," she said, "come to think of it." As if this had just now occurred to her.

The picture had its own private envelope. I slipped it out and turned it right side up. It was the kind of picture that hospitals used to give you, of a nurse wearing a surgical mask holding a sleeping, wrinkled infant.

"Where'd you get this?" I sat down on the edge of the sofa.

"I make friends," Mother said. "I talk to people."

I stared at the sleeping infant, wishing it would open its eyes.

They never showed me the baby in the hospital. Back then, they thought it would be harder on you. I suppose maybe today it's different. Most things are. They told me she was a girl, that she weighed six pounds something, and that she was perfectly normal, but that was all. I never asked to know anything more. I was just a kid myself, a schoolgirl. Since then, I have read novels and seen movies where these unwed mothers— cheerleaders and prom queens—suddenly develop super- human maternal instincts and fight like she-cats to keep their babies. All I can say is I never felt any of that. I felt like this thing had leeched into me and I couldn't pry it loose.

Your body recovers quickly when you're that young. Six- teen. I remember walking along the beach a few days after being released from the hospital, just bouncing around in the waves and screaming. The pure relief and joy of it. Suddenly I didn't even care that my whole life had been ruined, that my parents were disgraced and now separated as a result of my wantonness, that I didn't have a high school diploma, and that I'd only received one postcard from Tommy Boyd.

I wasn't even in love with Tommy Boyd. It happened the first and only time we ever went out. My boyfriend of two years had just thrown me over because I refused to do anything below the waist. I went to a friend's party with Tommy, hoping to make my boyfriend jealous, but when we arrived, the first thing I saw was him making out with Julie Mullins on the Mullins' riding lawn mower. (It was summer and the party was in the backyard.) I was so upset, I started drinking and flirting, and somehow I ended up in the back seat of Tommy's brother's car, doing everything. I was crying before he ever touched me. It started out as comfort.

The postcard was of the Painted desert. He and his older brother were driving cross-country that summer, disciples of Kerouac, before college started in the fall. In an exuberant scrawl he listed all the places they'd been. Then at the bottom, when he'd run out of room, he printed in letters nearly invisible to the naked human eye that he was thinking about me and hoped I was doing okay. He even called me from a pay phone once in California and held the receiver out of the booth so that I could hear the Pacific Ocean. I listened to the surf and sobbed for three minutes before the operator said our time was up. I try not to think back, but when I do, I don't blame Tommy Boyd. Never did. And I didn't blame my boyfriend because I loved him. Who I blamed was Julie Mullins. That is the way girls thought back then, before the women's movement raised their consciousness. It came too late for me. I feel closer to Tess of the D'Urbervilles than to Germaine Greer.

I handed the hospital picture back to Mother. We sat there for a minute listening to the geckos and the rain and the palm fronds scratching against the sliding glass doors. Mother picked up the remote control device and hit the "on" button. As the picture bloomed into view, I said, "Did I ever thank you for what you did? Taking me away and all?"

She just nodded and mumbled something, flipping through the channels. She settled on Masterpiece Theater. We had watched that episode together earlier in the week, but I didn't say anything. I picked the new *People* up off the coffee table and said I was going to read in bed. She nodded obliviously and then, just as I reached the hallway, she said, without taking her eyes off the screen, "You going to write to her?"

"Of course I am," I bristled. "I may be some things, but I am not rude."

"You going to invite them here? Her and the baby?" She swiveled her eyes sideways at me.

"I haven't thought that far," I said.

"Well, don't put it off." She slid her eyes back to the television. "She's been waiting twenty-five years."

I went to my room and changed into my nightgown. It was a hot, close night despite the rain, and I turned on the overhead fan. Mother and I dislike air-conditioning. A palmetto bug dropped off one of the blades onto the bed. I brushed him off, whacked him with my slipper, picked him up with a tissue, and carried him at arm's length to the toilet. I'd forgotten it was dark in the bathroom. I had to go back for the light bulb, climb up on the sink again, and screw in the 60-watt bulb. Crouched on the sink's rim, I caught sight of my face in the mirror and instinctively, like a baby, I reached out and touched my reflection. Then I brushed my hair and creamed my face, satisfied in the soft light that no one would ever suspect I was a grandmother.

The next morning by the time I had showered and dressed, Mother was already in the kitchen, eating her cereal. In the stark sunlight, she looked bad, worse than bad. The spoon doddered its way between her bowl and her mouth. The trembling spoon unnerved me. I feared it would not be long before I'd have to tuck a napkin under her chin and feed her like a baby. I felt my eyes swimming and stuck my head inside the refrigerator.

"You sleep?" I asked her. Mother and I are both thin sleepers.

I grabbed some oranges off the back porch and started to squeeze myself some fresh juice.

"I dreamed she came here with the baby. We were all sitting out on the lanai playing cards, even the baby. We had a special deck made up just for him. Only she . . . ," Mother hesitated to invoke her name, ". . . Linda Rose looked exactly like that dark-haired receptionist in Dr. Rayburn's office with the big dimples. Isn't that weird?"

"I've heard weirder." I tossed some cheese and crackers into a Baggie. "I'll be in the studio," I said. "You want anything before I go?"

Mother shook her head, dabbing at some dribbled milk on her robe. "I thought I'd just write some letters," she said. "You got anything for the postman when he comes?"

"No, I don't." I plunked her cereal bowl in the sink and sponged off the counter.

"You worried she's going to be trouble or ask for money? For all we know, she's married to a brain surgeon with his and her Cadillacs. Dallas is full of rich people."

"She didn't mention any husband at all," I said, getting drawn into it despite myself.

"Maybe you're worried 'like mother, like daughter.'" She was leafing through a rosebush catalog now, pretending non-chalance. "It's no disgrace these days, you know. Nowadays you'd be hard-pressed to think what you could do to disgrace yourself."

I lit a cigarette. Since Mother had to quit smoking, I tried to limit my smoking to the studio, but every once in a while she got on my nerves.

"Give me one," she said.

"You know you can't." I exhaled a smoke ring, followed by another one. They floated in the air like a pair of handcuffs.

"Just a puff," she pleaded.

Mother had smoked two packs of Camels a day for over thirty years. She liked to say that nothing could be harder than quitting smoking, not even dying. I put the cigarette to her lips and held it steady while she took a couple of drags. She closed her eyes and a look of pure pleasure stole over her features.

Then I felt guilty. "That's enough." I doused the cigarette under the faucet.

"Maybe you're worried she'll be disappointed in you," she said. "You know, that she's had this big fantasy for all these years that maybe you were Grace Kelly or Margaret Mead and who could live up to that? No one. But you don't have to, Fran, that's the thing. You're her flesh-and-blood mother and that's enough. That's all it'll take."

"Could we just drop this?" I wished I hadn't doused the cigarette. When she got onto some topic, it didn't make the least bit of difference to her if you preferred not to discuss it.

"You call me if you need me," I said.

She nodded and waved me away. When I looked back at her through the screen door, she was sitting there, frail and dejected, with those watery blue eyes magnified behind her bifocals, massaging her heart.

The studio was mercifully cool and quiet. I stared back and forth between the blue bowl of oranges on the table and the blue bowl of oranges I had painted on the paper clipped to my easel. I dipped my brush in water and mixed up some brown and yellow on my palette until I got the citrusy color I was after. I wondered if she, Linda Rose—there *was* something in Mother and me that resisted naming her after all these years— had inherited my eye. Maybe she had it and didn't even know it. Maybe she had been raised all wrong. Which was entirely possible, starting out with a tacky name like Linda Rose. She probably grew up twirling a baton and never even picked up a paintbrush. I would have named her something cool and elegant like Claire, not something that sounds like what you would call a motorboat.

As I focused on my oranges, the rest of my life blurred and faded away. I didn't give Linda Rose another thought that afternoon. Then I did what I always do when I finish a painting, my ritual. I lit a cigarette and sat in a canvas director's chair against the wall, facing the easel. As I stared at the painting, I gradually became more and more attuned to my other senses: the clatter of birds in the banyan tree, the salty breeze, the ache in my lower back, the taste of smoke. When I was satisfied that I was satisfied with the painting, I reached for the blue bowl, selected the most fragrant orange, peeled it, and ate it with slow deliberation, section by section, like some animal eating its afterbirth. Then I washed my hands and headed up the path toward the house to fix mother her lunch.

Mother was crying in front of the television set when I walked in.

"What happened?" I peered at the set expecting to see some melodrama, but it was just a quiz show. The contestants looked hypercheerful.

"I can't get this open." She handed me her painkillers, which were in a plastic vial. "You forgot to tell them no safety caps." Her quivering lips and trembling voice were a study in reproach.

"What if I did? It's certainly nothing to cry about." I pried the cap off and handed her the pills. "Here."

"I need some water."

I brought her a glass of water with a slice of lemon, the way she liked it.

"It seems like a little thing," she said, "but it's just one little thing after another. Like an old car. This goes, that goes. Pretty soon you're just waiting for the next part to give out."

"That's no way to talk," I said. "Come on now."

A couple of times she lifted the water glass up off the table and then set it down again as if it were too heavy.

"Here." I picked the glass up and tilted it to her lips. She took a few sips and then waved it away. Water cascaded down her chin.

"I don't believe in my body anymore," she said. "It won't be long now." She closed her eyes, as if she were trying out being dead. It scared me.

"I sure as hell don't know what's got into you," I shouted. I was rummaging through the kitchen cupboard. "You want Gazpacho or Golden Mushroom?"

"Don't shout," she shouted, motoring herself into the kitchen. "I'm not hungry."

I sighed and opened a can of soup. Even in summer, Mother and I live on soup.

"We're having Gazpacho," I said. "Chilled."

I poured the soup, threw an ice cube into each bowl, and stirred it around with my finger.

"I was thinking about what you'll do once I'm gone," she said.

I pushed her up close to the table, like a baby in a high chair. She ignored the bowl of soup in front of her.

"You've never been alone before. I don't like to think of you here all by yourself," she said.

"Maybe I'll like it."

"Maybe." She picked her spoon up and pushed it around in her soup. "But I doubt it. Just close your eyes for a minute and imagine this place is empty except for you. . . . Come on now. Close them."

"Jesus Christ." I sighed and slammed my eyes shut.

"How's it feel?"

"Peaceful." I glared at her. "Very peaceful." But, in truth, this shiver of loneliness rippled along my spine.

"You write to your daughter," she said.

Then, as if she'd exhausted that subject, she nodded off to sleep, wheezing lightly. When I turned my back to wash the dishes, her spoon clattered to the floor. I wanted to stuff her nylon nightgowns into an overnight bag and drive her to the hospital where experts would monitor her vital signs and, at the first hint of failure, hook her up to some mysterious life-support system until I was ready to let her go, but I simply picked her spoon up off the floor and rinsed it under the tap.

While Mother slept, I sat out on the lanai staring at a blank sheet of stationery until sunset. I had never been a letter writer. Even thank-you notes and get-well cards seemed to call for more than I had to say. Once or twice I'd tried to write a letter

to my father—in the spirit of reconciliation or revenge, de-
pending on my mood—but the words seemed to stick in my
mind. In the old days, when Mother still kept in touch with her
friends up north, I used to marvel at how she could fill up
page after page, her ballpoint flitting across the calm surface of
the scented page like a motorboat skimming through water,
her sentence trailing along in its wake like a water-skier holding on for dear life. Chatting on paper, she called it. I preferred
postcards. When Mother and I took a twelve-day tour of Europe for my thirtieth birthday, I sent back El Grecos from the
Prado, Turners from the Tate, Cézannes from the Jeu de Paume.
I don't have many friends, and those I have wouldn't expect
more than a couple of hasty lines on the back of a picture
postcard. Mother didn't even bother with postcards. Over the
years, her letters had shrunk to notes and then to nothing. At
Gatwick Airport, going home, I bought a biography of the
Duke and Duchess of Windsor to read on the plane. I have
since read everything I can find about them. I understand
them, but I don't pity them. Their fate was a simple equation.
When someone gives up the world for you, you become their
world.

I sat on the lanai for hours in the wicker rocker—the smell
of oranges from a bushel basket at my feet mingling with the
lilac-scented stationery—pen poised, trying to think what I
could say, what she would want to hear:

Dear Linda Rose,
   Last night I slept with your picture under my pillow. Every
year on your birthday mother and I would try to guess what
you looked like and what you were doing . . .

Dear Linda Rose,
   What is it you want from me? Our connection was a purely
physical one. I have never shed a tear on Mother's Day.

From behind me I heard the faint whir of Mother's electric wheelchair crescendoing as she steered herself down the hall and across the living room to the lanai. The blank white stationery looked gray in the dusk.

"Did you write her?" She was wheezing again.

"Yes." I shut the lid of the stationery box. "You take your medicine? You don't sound good."

"Never mind me. What'd you say? Did you ask her to come here?"

"Not exactly." It was cool on the lanai, a damp breeze from the ocean. I buttoned my cardigan. "Are you warm enough?"

Mother dogged me into the kitchen. I took a package of lamb chops from the refrigerator.

"Where's the letter?" She was sorting through some stamped envelopes, mostly bills, in a basket on the sideboard.

"I already mailed it." I stuck the chops in the toaster oven. "You want instant mashed or Minute Rice?"

"Don't lie to me." She jabbed me in the rear with her fingernail. "I'm your mother."

"Just leave me be." I turned the faucet on full blast to drown her out, muttering curses, but I knew she would wait. I shut the water off and set the pan on the burner to boil.

"Even half-dead I'm more alive than you are," she said.

In the bright overhead light she looked more than half-dead. She looked maybe 60 or 70 percent dead.

"You need a swift kick in the butt!" She wheeled her chair up behind me and tried to give me a swift one, but her toe only grazed my shin.

"Goddammit, I tried to write it," I said. "I kept getting stuck."

"I'll help you!" She stopped wheezing and something inside her rallied. Her spine snapped to attention. "I always could write a good letter."

I imagined I could hear her brain heating up, words hopping around in there like kernels in a popcorn popper.

"Get some paper and pencil!" she commanded. She was

chipping nail polish off her thumbs, something she did when she got worked up.

The chops were spattering away in the broiler. The water was boiling on the stove. "After dinner," I said.

The phone rang. I hurried out of the kitchen and answered it in the hallway. "Hello?" I said. There was silence, then a click, then a buzz. I hung up.

"Who was it?" Mother asked, as I set a plate of food down in front of her.

"No one. They hung up."

"I'm not hungry," she said.

"Eat it anyway." I dissected the meat on her plate into bite-sized pieces. "There."

After dinner, to make amends, I offered to paint mother's nails for her. Mother graciously accepted. One thing about her, she can recognize an olive branch. Her chipped purple nails looked unsightly in the 100-watt glare. She closed her eyes and swayed her head in time to the music on the radio. I shook the little bottle of Peach Melba and painted away with the furious effort of a child trying to stay inside the lines of a coloring book. My breathing slowed. My hands steadied themselves. My concentration was perfect, dead on. Nothing existed except the tiny brush, the shimmer of color, and the Gothic arch of each nail.

"What's that?" Mother said. She opened her eyes.

"Schumann, I think." I started on the second coat.

"Not that. I thought I heard a car door slam."

"I didn't hear anything."

A second later there was a loud pounding on the front door. It startled me and my hand skittered across Mother's, leaving a trail of Peach Melba.

"Told you."

"Whoever it is, we don't want any." I set the brush back in the bottle. "Religion, encyclopedias, hairbrushes . . ." I stood up and patted mother's hand. "Be right back."

"Don't unlock the screen door." She peeked through the drapes, careful not to disturb the wet nail polish. "Well, he's got himself a flashy car for a Fuller Brush man."

I put the chain on the door and opened it a crack. "Yes?" I said, peering into the darkness.

"Who is it?" Mother yelled from the living room.

"It's George Jeffries," a man's voice said.

I flicked on the porch light to get a good look at him.

"Who is it?" Mother yelled again.

I didn't answer her. A second later I heard the whir coming up behind me. She came to a stop right beside me.

"Hello, Lillian. I didn't mean to scare you," he said. "I would've called. I guess I was afraid you'd hang up on me."

"You're right. We would have." She was wringing her hands, smearing the nail polish all over.

"You could still slam the door in my face," he said.

"Good idea," Mother said, but I was already unlocking the screen door and motioning him inside.

The disturbing part was we didn't shout or cry or bare our souls to one another. We drank iced tea, then brandy, and conversed like three old friends who had lost touch with each other and were trying unsuccessfully to recapture something. Mother made a few barbed comments, tossed off a few poison darts, but my father just bowed his head and said, "You're right," or "I'm ashamed of myself," or "I deserve worse," and pretty soon she gave up. I could sense his shock every time he glanced at her. He didn't look that well preserved himself, but she could have been his mother.

I was mostly quiet. I couldn't believe that this thin-haired, mild-mannered old gent was my father. The main thing I felt was gypped. He told us how he'd been married again, lasted about eight years, then she left him. He wouldn't say who it was, but once he slipped and said Genevieve, and Mother and I exchanged glances. We knew it was one of her old bridge

Mama was smoking a cigarette and talking on Cody's toy telephone when Aunt Lucette and Uncle Bob came for us. We had our suitcases packed. I'd packed Cody's for him because he was too little to know what he'd need. Cody and I sat out on the front stoop while Aunt Lucette and Uncle Bob went inside to see Mama. Cody dug a tunnel in the dirt with an old spoon and I twisted my birthstone ring this way and that to catch the sunlight and make it sparkle. It was an aquamarine and my daddy gave it to me right before he ran off with my teacher, Miss Baker. After a few minutes, Cody got bored and went inside. I could hear them all fighting in there. Uncle Bob was shouting at Mama and then the screen door banged open and he threw Cody's toy phone out into the yard where it landed in the tall grass with a little jingle. Then Aunt Lucette swished out carrying Cody and hurried me into the car. Cody sat in her lap in the front seat and I sat in the back seat with my suitcase. Cody let loose with his tears, like a cloudburst. Aunt Lucette reached over and beeped the horn until Uncle Bob marched out and slid in behind the wheel.

"She's C-R-A-Z-Y," he said. "Breaks my heart."

He mopped the back of his neck with a handkerchief and started up the engine. I traced the letters on the side of my blue suitcase. I felt a little thrill. My daddy'd run off with my teacher and now my mama was crazy. I felt real special.

"She's skunk drunk," Aunt Lucette said. "She'd have to sober up to be crazy."

"We can't just leave her." Uncle Bob crossed his arms over the steering wheel and rested his head on them like he was about to take a nap. "She's liable to burn the place down with one of them fancy cigarillos of hers."

Ever since my daddy'd left, she'd been smoking these cigarettes that came in a flat box like crayons—pink and turquoise and purple. Sometimes she'd light one up and stand in front of the medicine chest mirror, watching herself smoke it down to a stub, and then she'd flush it down the toilet.

Uncle Bob shifted the car into reverse. "Maybe we should call a doctor," he said.

"She's heartsick and there's no medicine for that," Aunt Lucette sighed, "except time. We ought to know that."

Uncle Bob nodded and squeezed her hand. "Don't let's start," he said. There were tears shining in his eyes. I figured he was thinking about Little Bob.

As we pulled out of our driveway onto the paved road, I turned around and looked back at our house. Mama was kneeling in the tall grass that hadn't been mowed since Daddy left, clutching Cody's pink plastic phone to her chest. She saw me looking at her and put the receiver to her mouth like she was trying to tell me something.

Once we were onto the highway, we stopped for gas at a Sinclair station. I pointed out the green dinosaur to Cody who was only half-crying now. Uncle Bob told the man to fill her up, then turned to us and said, "Come on outta there. I wanna buy you kids a root beer."

We climbed out of the car and followed him over to the soda machine. I held Cody while Aunt Lucette went to the ladies' room. Uncle Bob dropped some change into the machine and handed me a root beer.

"You kids," he said, "is going to come live with us. Your mama's sick."

"How long for?" I asked, passing the root beer bottle to Cody.

"No telling," he shrugged. "Till your mama's her old self again."

"You poor kids." Aunt Lucette reached down and gave Cody and me a bear hug. "It's gonna be all right."

She took a pink Kleenex out of her skirt pocket and dabbed at her eyes. We climbed back in the car and I started whistling "You Are My Sunshine, My Only Sunshine." Daddy showed me how to whistle before he ran off and I'd been practicing up on some of the songs he used to like to whistle. Aunt Lucette swiveled her head around like Mama's old lazy Susan and looked at me like I was something real odd.

"Don't she beat all?" she asked Uncle Bob. "Not one little bitty teardrop. You suppose that's normal?"

"I expect it's the shock," Uncle Bob said.

I was whistling and watching the fields roll by. Some of them smelled real bad. I held my nose and breathed through my mouth. I saw a sign that said Welcome to Indiana.

"You know what, Cody?" I jiggled him on my lap.

"What?" He was half-asleep.

"We're in a new state." I pointed over my shoulder. "That back there's Kentucky." I pointed over the front seat. "And that up there's Indiana."

"I wanna go home," Cody whined.

"Look at my ring," I said, holding it eye-level so it sparkled right in front of his face. "See how pretty?"

He took his hand out of his mouth and tugged at my ring with his wet fingers.

Cody and I slept in the same bed at their house. At home we slept in the same room but in separate beds. We slept in Little Bob's room. In bed the first night I whispered to Cody about how Little Bob got run over by a bulldozer before Cody was even born. That made him remember his red dump truck my daddy gave him before he ran off, same day he gave me my ring. I'd set it out on the porch to take along, but at the last minute I forgot. Soon as he remembered it, I knew I wasn't going to get any sleep. Cody threw a fit and kept it up even when I lied and said we could go get it first thing in the morning.

The first week we stayed at home. I didn't go to school. Aunt Lucette was always asking me if I felt sad and telling me how it was good to cry.

"Cody cries enough for both of us," I said. "So does my mama. She cried for a solid week when my daddy ran off."

I polished up my ring with the hem of the tablecloth.

"Well, life can be real sad sometimes," Aunt Lucette said, her eyes filling with water. "There's no shame in crying." She looked at me like she was waiting for me to join in, but I just slid off my stool and went out the back door.

I liked sitting in the sun on the old aluminum milk box outside the back door. I'd sit out there with my eyes squeezed shut, pointing my face at the sun, whistling and rocking back and forth on the tin box. Sometimes, if no one bothered me, I could rock myself right into this trance. I felt like I just turned into pure sunlight.

The following Monday Aunt Lucette walked me to the school down the road from their house. She dropped Cody off at the neighbor lady's and we could hear him wailing for most of two blocks. We found the principal's office and I shook the principal's hand and told her my name was Heart Patterson and I was in the fifth grade. Then I sat on a bench and waited in the hall while Aunt Lucette told her all about me.

My new teacher, Mrs. Mitchell, was old and had a jelly belly. While she was writing spelling words on the board, I thought about how if I'd had Mrs. Mitchell back home instead of Miss Baker, my daddy'd still be home and my mama wouldn't be crazy. He met Miss Baker when my mama was down with the flu and he went to a parents' conference by himself. They brought in a substitute after Miss Baker and Daddy left town, but my mama kept me home from school. She said all the kids would be talking and making fun.

After Daddy left, Mama sat around in her bathrobe all day, not even combing her hair. She cried and watched the TV and drank Daddy's liquor. But one morning she took a bath, set her hair on hot rollers, then put on a fancy dress and painted herself up. She walked out onto the front porch where I was painting my nails. To keep Cody happy, I'd paint the nails on my one hand and let him blow on them. Then I'd do the same with the other hand. I was just starting in on my toenails when Mama sat down on the glider, smelling of perfume.

"Heart," she said, "do you think I look as pretty as Miss Baker?" She patted at her hair. "I want your honest opinion."

I looked at her for a minute, squinting and tilting my head. "No," I said. "But you smell real nice."

She slammed the screen door and locked herself in the bathroom. When she came back out, she was wearing her old bathrobe and no makeup. She didn't talk to me for two days. She'd say, "Cody, you tell your sister to bring me a beer," or "Cody, you tell that sister of yours she better run on down to the store and buy us some hamburger for supper." Then Cody'd turn to me real serious and say, "Buy hamburger."

I was the one who found the note my daddy left. My mama was at the hairdresser down the road when I came back home from school and found it under the saltshaker on the kitchen table. He wrote:

Dear Coral,
I won't be home for supper tonight or ever again. I never meant to hurt you or the kids, but I just can't help it. Fourteen years is a long time for two people like us to be married for. Maybe it's just too long. I don't want that you should be the last to know I'm taking Jean (Miss Baker) with me. She says Heart is a smart girl and she hopes Heart won't hate her now. We both feel sick about this. The money in the bank is yours and I'll send more on a regular basis. I got no intention of letting you starve. It's nothing personal against you, Coral. I never knew I was the type to do something like this.

I sat in the kitchen chair, shaking out little anthills of salt and pushing them around the flowered tablecloth till Mama came home. She set a bag of groceries down on the counter and took off her kerchief.

"Hi, Sunshine, you have a nice day?" She put some half-and-half in the refrigerator.

I shrugged.

Mama took some meat out of the bag. "You want pork chops or chicken for dinner?"

"I don't care." I turned my ring backward so that you couldn't see the stone and made a fist around it.

"You feel okay?" Mama studied me and rested her palm against my forehead like a cool rag.

"I'm okay," I said.

"Well, you look like you got a fever." She began stacking some fruit cocktail cans in the cupboard. "How was school?" she asked. "You like my new haircut?"

"Looks real nice," I said. "We had a substitute 'cause Daddy ran off with Miss Baker."

Mama looked at me like she was going to haul off and smack me. I handed her the note and ran outside. I started to skip rope as fast as I could. My feet hardly touched the dirt. As I skipped rope, I sang as loud as I could: "*A* my name is Alice, my husband's name is Albert, I come from Alabama, and I sell applejack." Whenever I had to stop to catch my breath, I could hear Mama inside cursing and crying up a storm. Once, when I was on *Q*, she called me to the porch and asked me had I ever seen my daddy with Miss Baker. I said no, and she went back inside and I picked up where I left off.

Once a week in my new school, Mrs. Mitchell would let me out of class for an hour so I could go talk to the school psychologist. He told me he traveled around from school to school, he was twenty-seven, and I should call him Jack. His office was the prettiest room in the school. The walls were bright yellow, there was a hooked rug like Grandma Patterson used to make before she went blind, and there were framed posters on the walls. Jack liked for us, him and me, to sit on big pillows on the floor, but I liked the wood chair. The first time I went to his office we sat on the big pillows and he explained to me that a psychologist was like a special friend. He told me I should feel free to say whatever popped into my mind. He said everything I told him would be a secret. I said okay, but I didn't have anything to say to him really. I'd just sit on the wood chair and look around at the animal posters till it was time to go back to class. Some days Jack would move my chair over by the window where there was this sandbox on legs filled with toys—tiny plastic adults and babies and animals and furniture and cars. He was always trying to get me to play with the toys and make up stories, but I didn't want to. I thought how my mama would like all those little toys, but I didn't say it out loud. I figured Aunt Lucette and Uncle Bob wanted to find out if I was C-R-A-Z-Y like my mama. That's why I was there. He even had a toy telephone hidden in a box of junk in the corner. There was a tambourine and an Etch-A-Sketch on top, but I spied the receiver dangling down the side of the box.

One night I had a dream our mama was lying in her bed with the house burning down around her. The firemen rescued her and took her to the hospital in an ambulance. When Cody and I visited her there, she was sitting all by herself in her yellow nightgown. The next morning at breakfast I asked Uncle Bob if Mama was in the hospital.

"Now where'd you go and get an idea like that?" he said. "Your mama's at home like she always was. She's just resting up."

"It's been a month," I said. "We gonna stay here forever?"

"Don't you like it here?" Aunt Lucette slid a pancake onto my plate. She looked like she was about to cry.

"I like it fine," I said. "I just like to know."

"Maybe this Sunday we could call your mama and you and Cody could talk to her. I bet she'd like that," Uncle Bob said.

Cody knocked over his milk and Aunt Lucette sponged it up.

"I don't want to talk to her," I said. I felt cold inside like I'd swallowed an ice cube. I jumped up and ran outside. I sat on my milk box and rocked real fast. I did this whenever I felt like crying and it worked real well. I never cried. I thought about my dream. Jack wanted me to tell him my dreams. Every time he asked me about them I said I couldn't remember. Sometimes I'd tell them to Cody when I woke up in the morning. Cody was always whimpering in his sleep like a dog. I was al-

ways shaking him awake. "Bad dream," I'd say. "Wake up."
Once he bit me in the shoulder during a bad dream—broke
the skin. When I snapped on the light, he looked like one of
those werewolves lying there sound asleep with my blood on
his baby teeth.

We got two postcards from our daddy in the same week.
One had a crocodile and the other was a map of Florida. He
said he was missing us and hoping we were taking good care
of our mama. He said he would send for us to visit him on
holidays just as soon as they found them a permanent place.
The postcards arrived in a white envelope with a letter from
our mama, but Aunt Lucette wouldn't let me see the letter even
though it had Cody's and my name on it. She folded it into
squares and slipped it into her brassiere.

"I'll tell Jack if you don't give me that letter." I looked her
straight in the eye.

Aunt Lucette flushed and looked all flustered. "Maybe I'll
just discuss the matter with him myself," she said. "If he says to
give it to you, then I will."

"Hmmmph," I snorted and stormed up to my room. I stared
at the ceiling and suddenly hoped that Jack would tell her not
to show me the letter. I'd seen this TV show where a crazy person sent a letter that was pasted-up words cut out of the newspaper. The words were all different sizes—some in tiny, thin
print and some in fat black print. The envelope my mama sent
had her fancy writing on it. Before my daddy ran off, my mama
prided herself on her round, curlicued handwriting. I thought
maybe my heart would stop beating if I opened up that envelope and saw those paste-up words.

While I was lying on the bed, Aunt Lucette knocked on the
door. She put a plate of home-baked gingersnaps and a glass of
milk on the bureau.

"I didn't mean to be mean to you, Heart honey," she said.
"I'm just trying to do what's best." Cody was dragging on her
skirt and she reached down and brushed his yellow hair out of

his eyes. "I know you miss your mama, but that's not your mama talking in that letter."

"Then who is it?" I reached over and took a cookie, still lying down.

Aunt Lucette was halfway out the door. "It's the fury of hell," she said. She put her hands over Cody's ears. "You ever hear that expression 'Hell hath no fury like a woman scorned'?"

"What's 'scorned'?" I was sitting up now. I had the feeling Aunt Lucette was talking to herself and once she remembered I was there she'd hush up.

"'Scorned' is like when you get tired of something and throw it away," she said. "You understand?"

"You take it to the dump," Cody piped up. Uncle Bob had bought him a new truck like the one we'd left at home.

"I understand," I said. I sort of did.

Aunt Lucette walked over and took the empty plate from the bureau. "You drink your milk up." She started out the door again.

"Aunt Lucette?"

She turned around and smiled at me.

"You keep the letter," I said. "I don't want it."

The next day I was sitting in Jack's office and he put the plastic dogs facing each other in the sand tray. "What do you think the dogs are doing?" he said.

I studied them for a while. "That dog there—the big one—is scorning that little dog," I said.

Jack looked surprised. Usually I didn't answer him when he asked me questions.

"Why's he scorning him?"

"It's not a him—it's a her." I pointed to the small white dog.

"Well, why's he scorning her?"

I shrugged.

"Those dogs remind you of anyone in particular?" He moved his chair closer to mine.

"No," I said.

"Maybe this big dog's sort of like your daddy?" He accidentally bumped his chair against the table leg and knocked the dogs over in the sand.

"Maybe." I picked up the white dog and set it on its four legs.

"Are you angry with your daddy?"

"No." I moved my chair back a little.

"Then why'd you leave him lying there in the sand?" He pointed to the big black dog.

I just looked at him. "My daddy's in Florida," I said. I squeezed a handful of sand, then let it sift out through my fingers. "In Florida the sand is hotter than this. It's like walking on fire."

"Actually it's not," Jack said. "It's white sand and it stays cool."

A bell rang. I could hear the chairs scraping and everyone's loud footsteps racing downstairs to the cafeteria. In a minute it was all quiet again, like a storm had passed us by. Jack patted my hand and smiled.

"When I say Florida, what's the first word pops into your mind?" he asked.

"Sunglasses," I said. I could see Daddy and Miss Baker driving in a convertible car wearing big sunglasses.

"What are you feeling right now, Heart?" His voice was soft and sneaky.

I looked out the window at the empty playground. One of the students had left his lunch sack by the jungle gym and some brown birds were pecking at it, pecking right through the paper.

"I'm hungry," I said.

After supper Cody and I were watching TV on the floor in the den when Uncle Bob came in and said, "There's someone on the phone wants to talk with you."

I went into the kitchen and Aunt Lucette kissed me on the cheek as she handed me the receiver. "Hello?" I said.

"Hello, Sunbeam, that you?"

"Daddy?" I put my hand over the receiver and whispered to Cody that it was our daddy.

"You get my postcards? I sent three so far," he said.

"We got them. You still in Florida?"

Cody was yanking on the phone cord. I shooed him away.

"We're in Tallahassee. I just found out this minute you been staying with Uncle Bob. You seen your mama at all?"

"No," I said. "She's crazy."

"That's no way to talk about your mama." He didn't say anything for a minute. "I know your mama. She'll snap out of it. You get your uncle to take you back home for a visit, you hear? Ain't nothing wrong with your mama that seeing you kids won't cure."

Cody was climbing on the kitchen chair, trying to grab at the receiver. "Cody wants to talk," I said. "He's talking real grown-up now."

"Okay. You tell your Uncle Bob I said to take you home," he said. "You kids don't never forget your mama and I love you."

"Here's Cody." I sat Cody down on the chair and handed him the phone. Then I walked out into the living room where Uncle Bob and Aunt Lucette were talking. They'd turned the volume down low. Aunt Lucette was twisting her Kleenex.

"Daddy says to tell you to take us home for a visit," I said. Then I turned the volume on the TV back up loud and lay down on my pillow in front of the set.

Saturday morning we woke up early, while it was still dark out, and threw our pajamas and toothbrushes in our suitcases we'd packed the night before. I was making up our bed when Aunt Lucette came in to check on us.

"You got Cody's toothbrush in there?" She walked around to the other side of the bed and helped me with the quilt.

"Yes."

"You excited?" she asked. "You glad we're going?"

"Guess so," I shrugged.

Aunt Lucette reached out and held my chin with her hand so I had to look right at her. "It worries me, honey, the way you act like nothing bothers you. You don't cry, you don't laugh.

Dr. Jack says you're just 'repressing' everything—you got all your feelings squashed way down inside you like a jack-in-the-box, and if you don't let them out bit by bit like a normal little girl, they're just going to pop out all at once some day."

Uncle Bob walked up behind her, pressing a little wad of bloody Kleenex to his chin where he'd cut himself shaving. "Everybody all set?" he asked, winking at Cody and me. "Don't fill her head up with all that psychiatrist talk," he said to Aunt Lucette. "She got troubles enough already."

Riding in the car I thought about what Aunt Lucette told me Jack told her. Cody and Aunt Lucette were snoozing. Uncle Bob was listening to the ball game on the radio. It was drizzling out and the car windows kept fogging up. I tried to picture my feelings all repressed together inside me—tears and laughs and frowns—trying to come out. I went limp and opened my mouth and closed my eyes and waited. I kept trying to coax them up, calling to them in my mind like you'd call a scared kitty. I pictured them flying up and out like a swarm of mad hornets. Then I pictured them floating up and out, nice and easy, like a row of bubbles. But nothing happened. I didn't feel a thing, except a little carsick. I wondered if Jack had actually said that about me. I figured Aunt Lucette must've got it all wrong.

I bunched my pillow up so I could lean my head against the window. I hadn't thought much about seeing Mama again. Uncle Bob said she was still sick, but he didn't want no one accusing him of keeping our mama from her kids. My birthday was next week. I was going to be eleven. This thought floated into my mind like a bubble that maybe this was my birthday surprise and when we drove up in front of our old house, Mama and Daddy would be standing out on the porch waving to us. Balloons would be tied to the porch railing, fluttering like butterflies in the wind, and inside there'd be a chocolate cake with pink marshmallow icing like I had last year, only with eleven candles instead of ten. Daddy'd be standing there with the camera while Mama lighted each candle with a match, trying not to burn her fingers. He'd be all ready to snap my picture as I blew out the candles and I wouldn't be able to think of anything to wish for.

Everyone was wide awake by the time we turned off the highway into Spottsville. Cody was standing on the seat looking out the window kind of puzzled. I think it was the first time in his life he was old enough to come back to a place he recognized. Aunt Lucette got her comb out of her purse and began yanking it through her hair. Then she handed it to me to do the same. When we turned down our street, we saw Farrah Hodge and Rusty Miller riding their bikes. They stared at us like they seen a ghost. Uncle Bob reached back and gave us two sticks of gum, the kind with sugar that Mama never let us chew. I put mine in my pocket. I didn't want to start off on the wrong foot with Mama.

Even from a distance, I could see there were no balloons. The grass still wasn't mowed and my daddy's red Chevy wasn't parked in the driveway. As we pulled up to the house, Uncle Bob cleared his throat and said, "Remember what I said, now. Your mama's still feeling puny. Don't take anything personal."

"Your mama loves you," Aunt Lucette said. "You just remember that."

We got out of the car and headed up the steps behind Uncle Bob. Cody's dump truck was lying right where I left it on the porch all rusted up.

"It's broke," he said like he was about to throw a fit.

"No it's not," I said. "That's just rust. Looks like a *real* dump truck now."

He brightened up and began playing with his truck. He'd forgot all about Mama and he hadn't even seen her yet.

"Anybody home?" Uncle Bob shouted and knocked on the screen door.

Mama walked out of the bedroom buckling her belt. She

had on her red party dress and high heels. She unlatched the screen door and we walked into the living room. Her dress was half-unzipped in the back. Aunt Lucette walked over and zipped it up. Mama said hello to everyone and sat down in the rocker. We sat across from her on the sofa. No one said anything for a minute. Then Uncle Bob said, "You're looking good, Coral."

"Am I?" Mama said.

"Real pretty," Aunt Lucette said. "Don't you think so, Heart?" Aunt Lucette jabbed me in the ribs.

"Real pretty," I said. "Prettier than Miss Baker."

Uncle Bob coughed and lit a cigarette. Mama started to cry. "You seen Frank?" she asked Uncle Bob.

"You know I haven't," he said. "I told you that on the phone."

Mama got up and went to the kitchen. We heard the refrigerator door open. I saw Aunt Lucette looking around the living room. It didn't look like Mama'd done much cleaning since we left. There were piles of dishes and magazines everywhere. I remembered how Mama used to yell at us for leaving a dirty glass or pair of socks in the living room and how she was always wiping this or polishing that, smelling of pine or lemon. She walked back in with a six-pack of beer, which she set down on the floor next to her rocker. She peeled off three beers and handed one to each of us. Aunt Lucette reached over and grabbed mine away from me before I had a chance to open it.

"Really, Coral," she said. "Where's your mind at?"

Mama opened her beer and took a long sip. No one said anything. Outside on the porch we could hear Cody yelling, "VVrrroomm, vroom! VVVrroommm, vrooooooommm!"

"It's Heart's birthday next week, Coral," Aunt Lucette said.

Mama didn't say anything. She took another sip of beer and spilled some down the front of her good dress. I got up and walked outside. Cody looked up from his truck.

"Mama's in there," I said.

He steered his truck across the porch to the door. He could just barely reach the door handle now on tiptoe. I reached over and held the door open for him while he vroomm-vroooomed over to Mama's rocker. I saw Mama reach down. I thought she was going to pat his head, but she just moved her beer out of his way. "Don't spill that," she said.

I stood on the porch watching the rain drip off the roof. I heard Mama say, "I saw Frank yesterday. He brought me some roses. He says he's tired of that woman." I heard Uncle Bob say, "You know you didn't see Frank, Coral. You know he's in Florida. You gotta snap yourself out of this. You ain't the only woman whose husband ever run off." I heard Cody making his truck noises. The metal wheels made a real racket on the wood floor. Mama yelled at him to watch where he was going. Then I heard Aunt Lucette say, "You've got to think of your children, Coral. The school psychologist says Heart is too withdrawn, she's like some walking zombie. He says she could end up real warped from all this."

I never heard what Mama said 'cause I went out into the yard. I held my arms straight out in front of me and stared straight ahead like my eyeballs were frozen. I walked back and forth across the yard with my arms and legs stiff as boards like the zombies I'd seen on TV. The tall grass wet my kneesocks. I felt my hair frizzing in the rain. From inside I heard Uncle Bob shouting and Cody howling. I got in the car and curled up on the back seat with my head on the pillow. The rain sounded loud beating on the tin roof of the car. I remembered my stick of gum in my pocket and unwrapped it. I had just popped it in my mouth when the car door flew open and Uncle Bob dumped Cody in the back seat. Cody's pants were soaked with beer and he smelled like a brewery, which was what my mama used to tell my daddy when he came home late. Cody was crying and Aunt Lucette was crying, but she looked mad, too.

"What happened?" I said, my mouth full of gum.

"She hit me," Cody said.

"Why?" I asked.

"She's crazy," Uncle Bob said and threw the car into reverse.

Uncle Bob backed up so fast we ended up on the lawn and heard a soft crack.

"Hope that wasn't a glass bottle," Aunt Lucette said.

"Jesus." Uncle Bob pounded the steering wheel with his fist. "Don't it never end?"

He got out and looked underneath the car. I noticed how my finger was turning green underneath my ring.

"Look at this." Uncle Bob held Cody's toy telephone up to the window for us to see. It was squashed like a pink pancake. Just as he was about to toss it back into the weeds, I rolled down my window and reached out my arm.

"Give it to me," I said.

Uncle Bob handed it to me. "What you want with that old piece of junk?" He got back in the car.

"I just like it," I said. "It's all repressed."

Uncle Bob shook his head and looked at Aunt Lucette. She reached over with her crumpled Kleenex and touched the little spot of dried blood from this morning still on his chin. Suddenly everyone seemed nice and calm, even Cody. Once we were out onto the paved road, I sat there staring at the telephone in my lap. It reminded me of those dead animals, skunks and squirrels, you see flattened on the highway. I picked up the receiver and tried to dial our home number on the mashed dial. "Hello, Mama?" I said. "This is Heart."

Uncle Bob turned the radio down. It was so quiet I could hear her breathing on the other end.

"I know you're there, Mama," I shouted. "You hear me?"

Cody looked at me like he'd never seen me before in his life. "Don't cry," he said. He reached over and touched me on the arm. "Don't cry."

Aunt Lucette handed me her Kleenex. Cody put his ear up against the receiver and listened, real puzzled, like maybe there was something he didn't understand.

The Rhythm of
Disintegration

All winter, from his office window in the Humanities Annex, Marshall has looked out over the frozen lake—Mendota or Monona, he can never remember which. All he knows for certain is that this lake is not the one in which Otis Redding's plane crashed. That was the other one, over by where his ex-wife lives in a large white cuckoo-clock chalet—the window boxes ablaze with healthy geraniums, like a travel poster of Switzerland. The beautiful and spacious house is so far from the rickety lower duplex Hannah and he shared in Berkeley it is as if she has been reincarnated into her next life while he is still living out his first. And in fact, when they talk—or try to—they are like two strangers who knew each other in a past life, a past life that he remembers and she chooses to forget—a willful amnesia that insults and saddens him. He has the sense that if it were not for Tilden, their nine-year-old daughter, his one living shred of proof, Hannah would cease to recognize him altogether. He wonders if it is something personal or if Hannah would treat Charlie, her new husband, with the same blank detachment were they to divorce someday. Of course *their* divorce would of necessity be more complex, a more substantial dissolution—houses, cars, antiques, a stock portfolio. Not like six years ago when Marshall remained in the duplex with the stereo, what passed as furniture, and Stokely—their aging Black Labrador, while Hannah moved back to Madison with their daughter, 1971 Datsun, and thousand-odd dollars in savings. At the time, Marshall consoled himself with the thought that she would regret it. Marshall regrets most everything he has ever done. He is a man full of regret, riddled with regret, but since returning to Madison, he has had to face the fact that Hannah not only does not regret, she does not even remember. Or so it seems. Or so she *wants* it to seem. Marshall's curse is that although he sees what's what, he always leaves the door ajar for hope.

The sun is shining, fierce against the large windows of his office, and the lake—Mendota or Monona—has nearly thawed, overnight it seems, into a surprising dazzle of blue. And now, after only a week or so of spring, Marshall finds that he can barely recall the long and brutal months of snow and subzero windchill about which he, a patriotic Californian, complained so relentlessly to whoever would listen. Already he doubts that the winter was really as bad as all that. It must be like labor pains, he thinks, looking at his watch. At noon he is meeting Hannah for lunch at the Memorial Union. It occurs to him to ask her whether she can remember her labor pains or whether it is simply another old wives' tale, but then he remembers she barely remembers *him*, their twelve years together, so it is unlikely she would remember anything so elusive as physical pain.

He has chosen the union over other more sophisticated restaurants because he hopes the familiar setting will jar something loose inside her. One sip of Rathskeller beer, and she will remember, suddenly *remember*, all the good times they had here, before the not-so-good times in Berkeley, and she will thaw, right before his eyes, like Lake Mendota or Monona. As he grabs his jacket, locks his office door behind him, and waits for the elevator, he feels hope fluttering its wings inside him, springing eternal, even though he knows that Hannah has only agreed, after some undignified wheedling on his part, to meet him today because he is leaving next week, his one-semester visiting lectureship ended, back home to California. The lunch is his reward for disappearing.

Keep it light, he lectures himself as he lopes down Langdon Street, past the tables full of jewelry from Nepal and thick bright sweaters from Colombia—just like Berkeley, like how Berkeley used to be before it went both downhill and uphill in the '80s. Today, walking past the tie-dyed T-shirt and candle vendors on his way to meet Hannah, he feels he has slipped into a time warp. He whistles and slings his tweed jacket over his shoulder, rolls up the sleeves of his pale blue shirt, imagining himself twenty years younger, knowing what he knows now, with an American Express card in his wallet.

Inside the union he weaves his way through throngs of students, gaudy and exuberant in the first heat of spring. A couple of attractive female students from his Historical Methods seminar call out his name and motion for him to join them. Flattered, he shakes his head, making a sad face and pointing to his watch as he continues on toward the terrace. Some days Marshall thinks becoming a professor was the most boorish choice he has ever made; other days it strikes him as a wonderful scam to get paid to monopolize the conversation, beautiful bright young women scribbling down your every word, the summers off.

He catches sight of Hannah sitting at a small table close to the lake. She answers his extravagant wave with a discreet nod and pulls her pocketbook tighter against her stomach, as if she expects him to make a grab for it or the sight of him makes her nauseated. He hopes that maybe she is just a tad nervous—butterflies—which would suggest that some atavistic memory is at work inside her, the place is working its magic. From a distance she does not look like her old self. Any number of girls sitting there in blue jeans and long straight pale hair look more like how she used to look back then. But as he threads his way toward her through backpacks and dogs and discarded trays, smiling self-consciously, he sees her face more and more clearly, her familiar distinctive expression, and he feels as if he is flipping the pages of a photo album backward. You would think up close the ravages of time would be more apparent, but in Hannah's case, somehow the opposite is true, as if she were just going through the outward motions of aging so as to fit in with Charlie and his crowd, who are considerably older, fiftyish, and obsessed with fitness. Once when Marshall brought Tilden back early and no one else was home, he'd persuaded his daughter to lead him on a tour of the house. The two things that most impressed him were the sunporch converted into a Nautilus home gym and the bookshelves full of crisp hardbacks at twenty dollars a shot, books that Marshall coveted in the bookstores but could not afford to buy until they came out in paperback. This was the straw of affluence that broke Marshall's back, and he'd left feeling depressed, a failure—angry at a society in which a cardiologist who never reads anything except the morning newspaper and the occasional best-seller on his annual vacation in the Bahamas can afford to stock up on hardbacks as if they were so many cans of soup.

Hannah has a half-eaten salad and a half-drunk glass of iced tea on the table in front of her. As Marshall sits down, she slides on some black sunglasses with mirrored lenses the color of oil slicks. The fact that she has not waited, that she is already halfway through lunch, irritates him. The message is as clear as if she'd spelled it out in salad dressing on the table. So much for his idle hopes of a lazy romantic lunch, the afternoon sun sinking into the blue lake as their conversation finally plunges into the past, the two of them as deaf to the hubbub around them as two sleek fish suspended, gliding in a shimmering deep-sea silence.

"Why are you frowning?" Hannah says, frowning herself.

"You could have waited."

She shrugs.

He jogs back inside the cafeteria, grabs a prewrapped sandwich and a bottle of beer, pays for them, and returns, breathless, to the table where Hannah is single-mindedly working away at her salad. As he unwraps his sandwich, she starts chatting about Tilden's new teacher, Mrs. Gorman, as if he has never met her, even though she knows perfectly well that Marshall has spoken with her on several occasions during the past four months when he picked Tilden up after school. As he listens to her rattle on, his fingers squeeze the cold sweaty glass of the beer bottle tighter and tighter, and he begins to make little revving noises in the back of his throat, which she ignores. The way her fork jabs at her lettuce reminds him of those clean-up guys who walk through public parks with sharp poles, stabbing at candy wrappers and used condoms.

This lunch was a mistake, he thinks, looking out over the water. He wants to interrupt, to say, Hey, remember the time we rented the canoe and capsized it? Remember this, remember that? But somehow it is not possible. Listening to her brisk small talk, he feels like a climber attempting unsuccessfully to find a toehold in a towering mountain of slick, hard ice. The air is thin, hard to breathe. He finishes off his beer and wants to go inside for another but is reluctant to leave even for a minute, afraid she will take this as her cue to make a swift and graceful exit. So what? What does it matter if she stays another five, ten, even twenty minutes? he asks himself, as he morosely peels the label off his beer bottle. What could possibly happen? What is it he wants to happen? He has a life in Berkeley, a fine life—tenure, a lover, a much-coveted apartment on Panoramic Way with a view of Alcatraz. He is even thinking of marrying again. In California he rarely gives Hannah a second thought. For the past couple years, he hasn't remembered their anniversary until long after it has passed. A phrase of Toynbee's from this morning's lecture—"the rhythm of disintegration"—suddenly lodges itself in his brain. He sighs and says he'd like another beer, can he get her anything?

Hannah shakes her head and says, as he predicted, that she really should go. He sighs again, more deeply, as she abruptly flings her napkin into her salad bowl and snaps, "What is it you want from me?"

Although this is the very question he's been waiting to answer, Marshall is rendered mute by her brusque exasperation. The tone is all wrong. The words crowd his brain, stampeding each other to get out, but his mouth is jammed shut, some sort of electronic failure of nerve. Finally he stammers, "I want you to take off those sunglasses."

Behind the mirrored lenses she glares at him and yanks open her large handbag. Marshall flinches, imagining for a moment that she is about to fling a handful of money at him, as if he is some persistent, pitiful beggar, but she extracts a piece of sunny yellow construction paper, folded in half, and hands it across the table to him. "From Tilden," she says. "A Bon Voyage card."

Marshall opens it and reads, printed in multicolor crayon: THIS SWISS MISS WILL MISS YOU. LOVE, HEIDI. He smiles and shows it to Hannah, who for the first time, it seems, smiles back.

"Those are my pet names for her," he says, a bit sheepish, "because she lives in a chalet."

"I know. She informed Mrs. Gorman she wants to be called Heidi from now on." Hannah shakes her head and laughs. They laugh together for an instant, Marshall stopping a beat too late, but in that instant he thinks he glimpses that tiny toehold.

"What I want from you," he says, leaning earnestly forward, "is a recognition of history, our history. You make me crazy the way you refuse to talk about, to acknowledge the past. I want to shake you. I want to shout. I want to drag you back there and make you see it." From the alarmed expression in her eyes, he can tell he is going too far, losing it. He lowers his voice and leans back in his chair. "A sense of continuity," he says more calmly. "That's all I want." Then, on an even lighter note: "You know how we historians are."

Hannah removes her sunglasses and studies him with narrowed eyes, as if to see less of him, or maybe she is just squinting in the bright sunlight. "I'm remarried. I have a new life." With an impatient flick of her wrist, she shoos an aggressive wasp away. "There's no room in my life for continuity if it means sitting around mooning over some romanticized version of the past with ex-lovers."

"Husband," he corrects her. "Ex-husband." As he says "ex," he sees himself sitting there, crossed out by a big red *X*.

She shrugs and snaps shut her handbag, a signal that she is about to leave. "Think of me like a house you sold. Someone else lives there now. You can't just barge in whenever you feel like it."

"You just don't get it, do you?" He sees her bristle, but the pedant in him blunders on. "Life is a process of accumulation, not substitution." He slumps in his chair, his posture an admission of defeat, waiting for the sound of her chair scraping against the concrete as she rises to go. At this instant he could kill her, bare-handed, without a shadow of remorse. She is like some willfully dense student who tunes him out, twists his words, refuses, out of spite, to understand. A fortress of vengeful, cold, unreceptive insensitivity. He can't believe he ever loved her, not for a single night. He closes his eyes, the sun battering against his eyelids, and tries to call forth a single heart-wrenching image of Hannah from the past, but there is nothing there—blank—like a tape that has been accidentally erased. Hannah says his name softly, nervously. He opens his eyes, blinking in the harsh light, and sees her shadow hovering over him, a dark avenging angel. If he stretched out his arm, it would slice right through her, through air, encountering no physical resistance, no corporeal reality. She is no more present in the present than in the past.

"Are you all right? Hey." She prods his foot with her toe as if he were a dead snake she fears might rouse itself for a final posthumous strike.

He nods untruthfully, dispirited, thinking he must find a new profession, which won't be easy at his age, forty-one. He sees himself, a defrocked priest of history, attempting to explain the reason for this career change to an executive headhunter. "I'm tired of looking backward," Marshall can hear himself saying. "The past is all washed up. I think maybe something high tech, something cutting edge." He will sublet his quaint apartment and move to some ahistorical condo in Silicon Valley. He will divest himself of the past, never eat leftovers, speak only in future tense. Yea, though I walk through the valley . . . He thinks of the quote from Lucretius he is using for the epigraph to his new book: *This is the sentence that has been passed upon the World; this is the law of God; that what*

has been must die, and what has grown up must grow old.
Suddenly he is trembling, shuddering, misfiring like a car with
dirty plugs. Hannah touches a fingertip to his eyelashes and
then says, "You aren't crying, are you?" as if she wants him to
deny it.

"Go," he says. "I'm okay. I just want to be alone." His voice
quavers, sullen and pitiful as a child's.

Hannah sits back down.

"I said I want to be alone," he repeats more firmly. He clears
his throat, sits up straighter, stares Hannah in the eye. "You can
go. Class dismissed."

But now there is no getting rid of her. She opens her handbag again, rummages around for a Kleenex, and holds it out to
him, a little white flag fluttering in the breeze. The symbolism
is not lost on him. He ignores her. She sets the Kleenex on the
table, where it promptly blows away.

"I'll get you another beer," she says, all conciliatory.

While she's gone, he thinks about leaving. He sees himself
standing up and walking out, stopping to chat wittily with the
two female students from his seminar. He doesn't know why
he doesn't. He really doesn't. A few feet away, two Middle Eastern students dressed like PLO terrorists are going through the
periodic table, no doubt quizzing each other for final exams.
KBr, NaCl. One corner of his brain translates wacky acronyms.
Killers for a Brighter Rehabilitation. National Association of
Chastened Lovers. Out on the pier, a black man is playing the
saxophone, a small white dog snoozing royally in the purple,
velvet-lined case. Sun, water. An academic resort. The antidote
to education.

In the distance, he sees Hannah walking toward him, a beer
in each hand, and he thinks maybe the lunch can still be sal-
vaged, maybe there's still time to get what he needs from her,
although he doesn't know what more he can say. Or do. And
already he regrets everything he has said or done thus far.
Hannah sets the two beers on the table and then tidies up,

moving all their trash to an empty table, wiping up some spilled salad dressing. A fit of wifely domesticity.

"Now"—she places her elbows on the clean table, leans toward him, lowers her voice conspiratorially, maternally—"tell me what's really the matter."

Marshall takes a long swig of beer and looks out over the lake, the sun glittering, a sea of jittering diamonds. Later, looking back, he will think to himself, half-joking, it was the sun, the sun made him do it, like Camus's Stranger—the sun, the saxophone, the Middle Eastern chant of the basic elements, the abrupt, dizzying shift from winter to spring, the bright beam of Hannah's sudden solicitude.

"You really want to hear?" he says.

She nods.

It is entirely unpremeditated. At first he has no idea where it even comes from. All he knows is that he opens his mouth and next thing he knows he is sitting right there listening to himself telling her this story, listening along with her, just as curious and moved as she, just as anxious to find out how it ends, more anxious, since it is (supposedly) his life, his love, his grief. Her sympathetic clucks and nods spur him on. When he sees tears glinting in her gray eyes, he feels so tender toward this fragile, bruised self he has created that he thinks he cannot bear it. The sadness is a thick, viscous liquid, sweet like maple syrup, drowning his lungs; congestive heart failure, the cardiologists—Charlie and his pals—would call it.

The story he tells her is this. About a year ago, after many years of living alone, Marshall saw a woman at the Café Med on Telegraph Avenue. A beautiful woman, naturally, as in most stories. She was drinking *café latte,* staring into space. Pale skin, huge dark eyes shadowed by dark circles. Marshall watched her for several minutes, transfixed, as he savored his *espresso.* Then suddenly, as if astrally projected, he felt himself drawn inside her. Never had he felt such grief, like an iron girdle squeezing his vital organs, every breath an intense effort. And then, just as suddenly, he was expelled—dizzy, buoyant with relief. As soon as he regained his composure, he stood up—without thinking, almost without volition—and walked over to her table. He waited. It took a moment for her to look up at him, then to bring him into focus, as if she were seeing him from a long way off. Looking into her eyes, he felt he was staring into deep water—anything could be down there—sunken treasure, shipwrecks, bloated corpses bedecked in pearls and coral. When he had her full attention, he said, "May I offer my condolences for your terrible sorrow." The woman's eyes filled with tears, and she motioned for him to take the empty chair across from her.

At this point in the story, Marshall catches his breath and sighs as it suddenly occurs to him where he has heard this story before: at a faculty cocktail party in Berkeley. A colleague in the French department. An anecdote about how André Breton had met his wife. The colleague, a svelte, worldly woman who had always rather intimidated Marshall, was wearing heavy, sweet perfume—gardenia, maybe, or nightblooming jasmine—and a low-cut black dress and was standing very close to him, almost whispering in his ear. He had definitely been aroused, although nothing came of it since he was there with Meredith, his lover, and a couple of days later he left for the Midwest. Telling the story, he seems to have conjured up the scent of jasmine. He sniffs the air, takes a sip of beer, disoriented.

"So what happened?" Hannah prompts him.

"We spent the night together." Marshall shrugs, as if to suggest the inevitability of it all. "She told me her husband and two children had drowned in an automobile accident, in Paris." He takes another slug of beer to give himself a moment—this is as far as the French professor's anecdote went. He was on his own now, but he found he didn't need time; the story seemed to have a momentum of its own.

"She moved into my place," he continues. "We were in love, perfectly compatible, content. After a few months, we decided to get married—in June." He pauses again, for dramatic effect, but when he goes on, he is surprised to find his voice choked up.

Hannah reaches across the table and grasps his hand. "Take your time," she commands gently. "There's no hurry."

"She died." He looks away, across the lake. The sax player, as if in accompaniment to Marshall's performance, has switched from cool jazz to blues. "An aneurysm. She was at a laundromat, the one on Euclid." Hannah nods. "Folding our sheets." Marshall is amazed at how these details just keep coming with no effort on his part. He remembers reading somewhere that the tiny unimportant details are what convince us something is true. Hannah and he are both silent for a moment, listening to the sax, the buzz of conversation at the neighboring tables that seems suddenly to increase in volume, the tinny yap of the sax player's dog—like one of those wind-up toys. Watching the dog, Marshall feels that some inner mechanism of his own, previously wound tight, has abruptly unwound.

"I'm sorry," Hannah says finally. "I had no idea."

Marshall busies himself with his beer, self-conscious now and feeling rather foolish, as if he has just emerged from an autohypnotic trance, but there is also a sadness, a deep ache, lingering inside his chest as if from an old wound. He remembers a Vietnamese student of his whose index finger was amputated at the knuckle. One day Marshall had finally asked him what had happened to the finger, and the student had said he didn't know. He had been an orphan, adopted at a young age by an American family. He had no memory of the finger and no one to ask. As he spoke, he'd stared at his maimed hand matter-of-factly, but Marshall had been haunted by the story, still often dreamed some gruesome version of it. Imagine, he'd said to Meredith in bed that night, having part of your body missing and not knowing why, how, when.

Looking at the sax player's dog, Hannah suddenly smiles and says, "Remember the day Stokely rolled in horseshit at

Hilmar's farm and we took off all our clothes and took turns hosing him down?"

Marshall holds himself very still and just barely nods his head, not daring to look at her, not daring to breathe, hoping that she will continue.

"That was a nice afternoon," is all she says after a long silence.

He releases his breath in what sounds like an exaggerated sigh of disappointment or boredom, which causes Hannah to frown and fiddle with her wedding ring.

"I can't picture Charlie running around naked after a stinky dog," he says, attempting a good-natured laugh. To be honest, he can't exactly see himself doing such a thing these days. Even if Stokely were still alive.

Hannah shrugs and takes hold of his wrist, turns it to see the time. "I really do have to go. Tilden will be home from school soon." She slides her sunglasses on again and stands up. "Walk me to the bus stop?"

"I'll give you a ride." He stands up too, then says, "Wait a second. Be right back." He jogs down to the pier and tosses a five-dollar bill into the purple velvet case. As Marshall turns to go, the sax player makes a courtly bow in his direction and plays a flashy riff.

Hannah takes his hand companionably as they walk toward the Humanities Annex, where his car is parked. For the first time in the four months he's been here, he does not feel like prodding and shaking her. He is in a strange mood, hard to define—a moodless mood. He feels oddly displaced. As he makes small talk, he has the sensation that his lips and words are out of sync, but Hannah doesn't seem to notice. Every now and then she gives his hand a gentle maternal squeeze, as if to let him know she has not forgotten his terrible loss. Surprisingly, he feels no guilt, no regret, over his elaborate lie, no need to confess. Deep down he feels entitled to this consolation; he drinks it up like a thirsty brown-edged fern.

In the car, during the short drive to Hannah's house, they listen to a tape Marshall has just recently bought—*Otis Redding's Greatest Hits*. Hannah sprawls in her seat, one foot resting against the dash—an unladylike posture for a doctor's wife—and as they cruise down John Nolan Drive past the other lake, Monona or Mendota, it could be 1970, Marshall thinks. They could be in love. Or think they were. Marshall wonders if they ever were really. He hopes so, he really does. But as he pulls up in front of the white chalet with its cheerful geraniums, he has the sudden sad conviction that what Hannah and he had was just puppy stuff—wriggling, yapping, licking, biting—whereas Hannah and Charlie have the full-grown dog: he pictures two loyal and patient Golden Retrievers lying side by side on a stone hearth, year after year, their muzzles slowly turning white.

Hannah leans over and kisses him lightly on the cheek. "Call before you leave?"

He nods. "I'm taking Tilden to the movies Saturday. Thanks for lunch." He gives her a stiff hug. Over her shoulder he can see the lake, the one where Otis's plane crashed. The news has been full of Otis lately. Some organization raising money to erect a memorial on the shore of the lake, the twentieth anniversary of his death. "Is this Mendota or Monona?" Marshall asks as Hannah opens the car door.

"Monona," Hannah laughs.

"Monona," he repeats, determined to remember this time.

After Hannah disappears inside the house, he sits there in the car, looking at the lake and listening to the tape, tapping his fingers against the steering wheel in time to the music. Just sitting on the dock of the bay. He imagines Otis sitting in his plane at the bottom of the lake, perfectly preserved, like a ship in a bottle. Then he realizes that, in fact, he is picturing the black saxophone player, and when he tries to picture Otis's face, there's nothing there—a blank. Suddenly he feels depressed, more depressed than he has ever felt in his life, grief-stricken. It is as if his story, his lie, has solidified into truth. He loves that woman with the drowned husband and children, loves the distracted way she sips her *café latte*, loves her sad dark-circled eyes, loves the way she folds their bed sheets— smoothing the wrinkles as if love depended on such small gestures. He wants her back more than anything he has ever lost, anything. He would do anything to get her back. He holds his index finger out straight against the steering wheel and thinks of his Vietnamese student and of his old friend TJ, who axed off his little toe to get out of the draft. He would do that, he thinks, for her, and not even feel it. He closes his eyes and pictures her and suddenly he recognizes her—or not so much recognizes her as knows who she is, why she looks so familiar. A little bit like Hannah around the mouth, like his high-school sweetheart around the eyes, even a bit like his mother—not as she is now but as he remembers her from his childhood, with a cloud of dark hair brushing his cheek, tickling him, as she bent over to kiss him good-night. The woman is the original loss, the mother of loss, the Ur-loss, the loss from which all subsequent losses flow, as if it is just one loss in different guises—all our lives—we lose the same thing over and over and over.

Hearing the crunch of tires on gravel, Marshall opens his eyes and quickly slides down on the seat as Charlie's silver Porsche sails into the driveway just beyond where Marshall is parked. In the late afternoon sunlight the silver car silhouetted against the deep blue lake shines like a shark. Slumped in his seat, Marshall watches as Charlie jaunts across the velvety green lawn, whistling like a man happy to be home after a hard day, a man with no regrets in the world. At the porch steps, he bends down and fiddles with something in the bushes. As he enters the house, shutting the front door behind him, a half-dozen sprinklers burst into action, whirling and sparkling away, cascading into the open window of Marshall's car, soaking his shirt and pants. He curses and rolls up the car window.

The sprinklers beat like heavy rain against the glass and he feels strangely disoriented, unreal, sitting there in the rain on a sunny day, like a movie actor on a sound stage. He remembers the tour Hannah and he took of Universal Studios the first summer they lived in California—simulated thunder, rain, lightning, even snow. He remembers that after the tour they drove out to the beach and had dinner with Hannah's old boyfriend and how upset he, Marshall, the current boyfriend, had been while Hannah and Rick had gossiped about old friends and laughed at in-jokes that had to be laboriously and unfunnily explained for Marshall's benefit. He wonders why it is that he and Hannah can't go to restaurants and laugh at injokes that they have to stop and explain to Charlie. He feels cheated, shortchanged, as if the past were a joint savings account that Hannah had unilaterally closed out. He wants to protest this unfairness, wishes he could haul her into small claims court and force her to give him what he wants. Which is what? What is it you want from me?—Hannah's question again. He knows exactly what it is he wants, but somehow he can't find the words to describe it. The words he tries and rejects all make it sound like both more and less than what it really is: an acknowledgment of loss. "If we lose the loss," he hears himself saying to her, "then what's left?" He thinks of simulated snow drifting prettily, like a sheet of blank paper.

It is hot and steamy in the car. He rolls down the window and lets the cool spray of the sprinklers wash over him. He rests his head against the back of the seat and shuts his eyes for a moment, tired. When he opens them again, Tilden is standing there staring at him. "Daddy," she frowns, exactly like her mother, "what are you doing? You're all wet."

"I'm waiting for the rain to let up," he says.

She considers this seriously for a moment and then smiles, as if she has just figured out the punch line to the world's most amusing joke, a little in-joke just between the two of them. Squinting into the bright haze of sunshine, she opens up an imaginary umbrella, then saunters around to the other side of the car and climbs in. "I'll wait with you," she says.

He flips over the cassette and snaps on the windshield wipers. Tilden giggles and waves to Hannah, who is watching them from an upstairs window, half-smiling. Marshall flashes her a peace sign. She laughs and flashes one back, then lets the curtain fall forward and disappears. There is a sudden loud clap of thunder, a flash of heat lightning. Tilden leaps onto his lap. He wraps his arms around her tight and sniffs her clean shiny hair, child's hair. It must be hereditary, he thinks, remembering Hannah's fear of thunderstorms, how she used to take her pillow and sleep in the hallway, away from all the windows. The thunder rumbles in the distance. Tilden shivers against his chest. He cranks up the volume on the tape deck. Otis is singing about tenderness, wailing, screaming his lungs out, like a dead man shouting to be heard.

Eating Alone

Driving home from my sister Delphine's funeral, I suddenly got hungry. I got hunger the way some people get religion. It was like the Holy Ghost entered into me and he had not eaten a square meal in years. Then, not five minutes later, even though there had been nothing but scrub fields for miles and miles, I spied a Howard Johnson's in the distance, perched on a stark hill, seeming to float and shimmer in the midday heat. I took the next exit.

It was July. The parking lot was jam-full of dusty cars loaded down with inner tubes and bicycles and hibachis. Death takes a holiday, I thought, even though it didn't make much sense— just one of those phrases that suddenly lodges itself in your brain like a kernel of corn between your teeth. Stomach growling, I waited impatiently for a sports car to back out and then cautiously inched my old Nova in between two station wagons. I turned off the engine, kicked off my rubber flip-flops, and eased my heat-swollen feet into a pair of open-toed pumps. My poor feet looked like two twice-baked potatoes.

Once inside the air-conditioned restaurant, I sat down in a booth and stared at the color photos of fried clams and veal parmigiana until I surprised myself by standing up and waving my arms to get the waitress's attention. Usually I am the patient and undemanding type. The waitress took one look at me and hurried over with a glass of ice water.

"I'll have a cheeseburger, a clam roll, some onion rings, and a chocolate shake," I fired off before she'd even got her pencil poised. My hands were trembling.

The waitress looked at me and said, "You all right, honey?"

"I'm just a touch diabetic." I smiled and tucked my hands between my knees.

Her eyebrows shot up in alarm, as if she expected me to slip into a coma on the spot. "Well, you just hang in there. I'll be back with that shake in two shakes." She hurried off.

The instant she left, I stopped trembling, as if the little lie had somehow steadied me. It was Delphine who was the diabetic. She used to shoot herself up every morning. I never could stand to watch. Delphine always said that's how she would go—a diabetic coma—and she was right. I always said I thought I'd go in an airplane crash, but I didn't really think that. I rarely flew, and I just had the sense that however I died, it wasn't going to be the kind of death that makes the evening news. It would be quiet, slow, and painful.

The waitress bustled back with my milk shake and promised the food would be out in a jiffy. I smiled and thanked her. By the time she got back to the booth with my cheeseburger and onion rings, I'd polished off the milk shake. I ordered a large Diet Coke and a slice of Black Forest cake and attacked my cheeseburger. I felt as if I'd been hollowed out like a plucked turkey on the inside, and in fact, I could not remember eating a single meal since Delphine's husband, Russell, had called me with the bad news, four days ago.

He got as far as, "Georgina, it's Russell." Then his voice broke up and he had to hand over the phone to Noelle, the older daughter, age thirteen, to give me the details. She was crying too, but in a more restrained fashion. After I hung up, I sat there waiting for it to hit me. Delphine is dead, I repeated over and over in my mind, enunciating each word clearly. It was like some common phrase I had memorized in a foreign language and then promptly forgotten its meaning. I sat there until it was time for the evening news and then I walked over and turned the television set on. Delphine had always occupied such center stage in my mind, it was hard to believe that she was not a celebrity, that her passing did not merit so much as a single line from CBS.

Later that same night, lying alone in bed, I had managed to cry finally, but what started me off was not thinking about my sister so much as thinking about myself. I kept hearing Russell and Noelle crying long-distance into the receiver, and I lay there in the dark wondering if, when my time came, there would be enough tears to fill up a shot glass. Delphine and I had always been competitive like that. Being the oldest, she got the best of everything first. It was just typical of the way things always worked out between us that I was there to mourn for her, but where would she be when it was my turn?

The waitress cleared away my empty plates and set down the Black Forest cake. Trying to ignore the fact that it tasted like some Hollywood prop, I ate it right up. When I was done, I didn't feel so good. I left the waitress a big tip and visited the ladies' room on the way out. For a minute I thought I might be sick, but then it passed and I felt all right again, just a little bloated. I loosened my belt and splashed cold water on my face. As I held my hands under the blow-dryer, I suddenly remembered seeing Bonnie, Delphine's younger girl, sitting on the edge of the bathtub, pointing the pink, gun-shaped blow-dryer at her face. At first I'd thought she was drying her bangs, but then I noticed her shoulders shaking and saw that she was drying her tears. The others were already in the air-conditioned car, baking in the hot sun on the driveway, waiting to go to the church. Although I had been sent inside to hurry her along, I just tiptoed back down the hall without saying a word. I went back outside to the car and said to Russell, "She's crying in there."

He looked up at me and frowned, as if trying to figure out how such a lush passionflower as his Delphine could have been related to such a stiff thistle as me, who did not even know how to comfort a crying child. Then he nudged the air-conditioning up a notch, sighed, and said to Noelle, "Go tell your sister to get her butt out here."

Noelle heaved a sigh right back, stuck out her lower lip, and dragged herself out of the car toward the house. When she got to the front door, she whirled around and glared at us. Russell smacked his fist into his palm, mumbled some curses, and then rested his forehead wearily against the steering wheel with a soft whimpering moan. I sat there frozen with embarrassment for a moment. Then, melted by a sudden flame of tenderness, I stretched my hand forward from the back seat, and just as it gingerly alighted on his broad shoulder, an explosion rocked the car. I snapped my hand back and Russell jerked up like he'd been shot. "Goddamn Jesus fuck!" he pounded the dashboard. Then he twisted himself around and said, "Air-conditioner blew out. You okay?" I nodded shakily. The girls came running out of the house and stood there clinging to each other like two shell-shocked orphans on the evening news.

Standing there in the ladies' room, remembering the look on those little girls' faces, it was suddenly clear to me what I had to do, like it or not. What I had to do, it seemed, was turn that car around and drive the two hundred miles back to Delphine's house in Lebanon, Florida. Those little girls needed me. Not to mention Russell. And after all, who was waiting for me back home?

Out on the highway, heading back down south, I unwrapped a butter-rum Life Saver without taking my eyes off the road and popped it into my mouth. Fifteen years ago, fumbling around for a lit cigarette he'd dropped between his legs, my husband had smashed his new Oldsmobile into a telephone pole. I know this for a fact because the girl in the passenger seat "survived with only minor bruises and lacerations," as the news reporters always say. When I visited her in the hospital, she said she was just a hitchhiker, and I believed her. Earl and I had only been married fourteen months. But when I was sorting through his things, I came across a strip of those photo-booth photos—the kind where you pay a dollar (fifty cents back then) and crowd into the little cubicle together and close the curtain and make silly faces. She was sitting on his lap and he had his arm inside her sweater, his hand waving naughtily to the camera from the V-neck, his bony wrist sandwiched between two slices of Wonderbreast. I tore the photos up, flushed them down the toilet, and never told anyone about finding them, not even Delphine. Especially not Delphine. No man had ever been unfaithful to my sister. She was the type that inspired instantaneous lifelong devotion. At her funeral I had counted three ex-boyfriends sitting toward the back, looking like they had just been stood up for the senior prom.

It was evening, dinnertime, when I pulled up in front of Delphine's house—a modest, ordinary house except for Delphine's crazy quilt of bright flowers presided over by a large stone Buddha, hands resting palms-upward on each knee as if waiting for the first raindrops to fall. Even though there was room in the driveway next to Russell's old Thunderbird, his pride and joy, I parked my car across the street and watched the still, silent house, as if waiting for some sign. Now that I was actually back, I suddenly felt shy about announcing my arrival. I wanted someone to look out and notice me there and come running to drag me inside. But no one did. And for an instant, sitting there in my parked car, squinting as the setting sun glinted off the T-bird's shiny chrome, I felt a stab of jealousy just as sharp and bright as the afternoon I had first glimpsed Delphine smoking a cigarette and laughing in the passenger seat next to Russell. Not that I had any claim on Russell. He was just someone I had always daydreamed about in my younger days, before I'd married and moved away, for good I'd thought. But just two years later, there I was again—back home in West Virginia—a widow taking care of my widowed father. An emotional wreck nursing a physical wreck. Life didn't seem to hold much promise for me. And as I walked out of Charmer's Pharmacy, where I had gone to get our father's prescription refilled, there was Delphine, a stewardess home for the holidays—in between Paris and Tokyo—cruising by with a handsome man, a golf pro, in a turquoise Thunderbird. I waved but she looked right through me. Just like that stone Buddha, only smiling.

The last fierce rays of sun were sinking behind the house. It was hot and I was tired from all that driving. I turned on the car radio and popped the last Life Saver into my mouth. For a panicked instant I thought, what if they've gone away somewhere, but then I thought, don't be silly. Russell would never go off and leave his T-bird sitting out like that, exposed to the elements. In Charles Town he'd used a canvas cover to protect against the snow, and Delphine had teased him about tucking his car into bed for the night. I sighed and rested my head against the seat for a moment. As I shut my eyes, I had a clear image of a Christmas card Delphine had sent me a few years back—a snapshot of the four of them in bathing suits, patting handfuls of some white, fluffy substance (shaving cream? mashed potatoes?) onto the stone Buddha, who was sporting a snowman's plaid scarf and hat.

When I woke up, it was past midnight and I was hungry again—as if I'd eaten Chinese food for lunch. Travel must have scrambled my metabolism, because normally I am on the scrawny side with an indifferent appetite. After Earl died and I was alone again, I stopped cooking all those big dinners and lived on cottage cheese and canned Mandarin oranges for weeks. Sometimes I would get into bed at night and I could not even remember if I had eaten dinner or not. I would have to get up and go out to the kitchen and look to see if there were any dishes in the sink. I was still living in Long Beach, where Earl had whisked us off to, and as I looked at the dishes in the sink, I always thought of this dim sum restaurant in Chinatown Earl had taken me to once where there were no set prices—they figured out how much you owed by counting up all the little saucers on the table.

My muscles were all cramped up from sleeping in the car, my dress was stuck to me like wet toilet paper, and I could taste my own sharp sweat in the back of my throat. I got out and stretched and tried to think what to do. My bladder felt about to burst. The lights in the house were all off, and I couldn't see myself knocking on the door, rousing everyone in the dead of night. The gas tank was on empty and the nearest motel was back out on the highway. My stomach rumbled. Out there alone in the dark it had that mournful sound of a train roaring through vast open spaces.

Feeling like a burglar, I closed the car door softly and cut across the lawn. The front door was locked tight. My bladder was screaming. I hurried around back and tried the back door. The screen was latched. I couldn't hold it any longer. I squatted in the corner of the yard by the hibiscus hedge, yanked down my underpants, and let loose a hot splashy stream onto the cool, green grass. I have to admit I enjoyed it. I felt as if I were three years old again, being led all over the neighborhood by Delphine, who liked nothing more than squatting behind bushes and peeing anywhere but in her own toilet. The more public the spot, the more chance of getting caught, the more thrill she got out of it. Once, when she was seven or eight and I was four or five, she took me and the Dietz twins into the woods and ordered us to dig a little ditch, which she called a latrine, and told us she'd give us each a Bit-O-Honey if we pooped in it. When Buddy protested, she told him it was what soldiers did. Then she walked back and forth, swinging a pussy willow branch, as we dutifully squatted on our haunches, straining to please her.

Moonlight shimmered on the calm surface of the little swimming pool. The thought of how refreshing a cool dip would be suddenly distracted me from my hunger. I hesitated for a moment, then tugged off my sweaty dress and underwear. Delphine would approve, I thought, as I eased myself into the lukewarm water. She was always a great one for skinny-dipping, always the first one to shed her suit at the rock quarry, throwing the rest of us girls into an agony of embarrassed indecision. Unlike Delphine, who seemed to glory in her femaleness, I felt my breasts were silly and conspicuous and foreign, like a bad toupee. When boys petted them, I felt nothing. They might as well have been tickling an artificial limb. Until I met Earl. Earl had a way about him. The first time we made love it was as if he saw my mind up there glaring down at us like a harsh overhead light, and he just reached up and snapped it off, and I thought, so this is how it's supposed to be.

I was breaststroking back and forth across the small pool,

enjoying the languid movement after a full day in the car, when the back door suddenly flew open and a floodlight burst on and Russell's shaky voice hollered out, "Delphine? Is that you?"

Before I could answer, he jumped into the pool stark naked and swam toward me. I screamed and started thrashing in the other direction. It was a small pool. He reached out and grabbed my ankle and towed me in. My head was underwater, so I could not shout without choking. I tried to kick him loose, but he was all over me like an octopus. Finally he turned me around and raised my head up out of the water, and as he leaned toward me, I could smell he had been drinking. I ducked my head to the side so his lips just grazed my cheek and said, "It's Georgina, Russell. Your sister-in-law."

He let go of me then and actually wiped his hand across his mouth. It hurt my feelings. "Jesus Christ," he groaned. "What the f——" He plunged himself down into the water and crouched there, holding his breath. The floodlight was shining, and although I felt uncomfortable standing there naked in the pool, I felt even more uncomfortable about climbing out.

"You think you could turn out that light?" I said when he surfaced again.

I turned my back as he heaved himself out of the pool. His wet feet slapped against the cement, and an instant later it was blessedly dark. The screen door banged open and shut. Alone again, I scrambled up the chrome ladder and into my clothes. I wrung my hair out and stood there uncertainly, feeling disgraced and disheveled, wondering how things could have got off to such a bad start. I was considering just getting back in the car and driving off when the screen door screeched open again. Russell had put on some shorts and he was waving a towel at me.

"You going to stand out there all night?" he said.

I gave my hair one last vicious squeeze and headed toward the house. At the door he handed me the towel and said, "You want a drink?"

Before I could answer, he was at the counter splashing gin

into two glasses. It seemed to me he had already had plenty, and it occurred to me to hope that maybe he would not remember anything in the morning and we could start fresh.

"Thank you." I took the glass he offered and took a sip, surprised to find how thirsty I was. From the other room, I could hear the drone of the TV and realized he must have been awake all the time, sitting there in the dark. Crouched in the unflattering light of the open refrigerator, he was piling sandwich makings on the counter. For the first time I noticed his blond hair was thinning on top. This touched me. If I could have siphoned Russell's sorrow from his tank into mine, I would have. The bread was sitting in a pool of spilled gin. I reached over and moved it to higher ground. Then, for something to do, I started assembling the bread, bologna, and cheese. He handed me the mustard. The jar was almost empty. Suddenly, as I maneuvered the knife around inside the jar, it hit me how Delphine had no doubt bought this jar of Dijon mustard never thinking for an instant that it would be the last jar of mustard she would ever buy. And I thought about how the house was filled with things Delphine had bought that would gradually be used up and replaced with things her hands had never touched. The girls would outgrow the clothes she had bought them and pick out new ones she had never seen. The sheets on their queen-size bed would wear out and Russell would sleep on sheets she had never felt against her bare skin. Bit by bit she would disappear until there was not a trace of her left.

Russell was sitting at the table, head down, pressing his cool glass against his forehead as if he had a headache. "She used to do that. Nights when she couldn't sleep." He sighed. "I'd wake up. The bed would be empty. And I'd hear her out there swimming in the pool."

I plunked a sandwich down in front of him. He looked up at me, surprised and bleary-eyed, as if he had forgotten I was there, as if he were just talking to himself.

"Eat," I said. "You need it."

He took an obedient bite out of his sandwich, set it down, lifted the top slice of bread, and frowned.

"Something wrong?" I said.

"Needs more mustard."

I scraped the very last bright traces of mustard from the jar and tossed it into the trash basket. "Okay?"

He nodded.

There was a small blackboard stuck to the refrigerator. It said *tin foil, napkins, garlic.* I picked up the miniature eraser, wiped off Delphine's flamboyant scrawl, and printed *mustard.* Then I sat down at the table across from Russell. "I thought I'd stay and help for a while," I said. "The girls need someone. Just until you're all back on your feet." I fished the lime wedge out of my drink and sucked at it. When he didn't say anything, I added, "I'm certain Delphine would have done the same for me."

Russell nodded and stood up, staring down at me with a glazed, panicky blankness, like an actor who can't think what comes next.

"You go to bed," I said. "I'll just clean up here."

As soon as he'd gone, the kitchen seemed bleak and spooky. The dead middle of the night. As I rinsed Russell's plate and our two glasses and placed them side by side in the drainer, I kept glancing over my shoulder, half-expecting Delphine to bustle in and shove me aside. Then I took a careful inventory of the empty refrigerator, rummaged around in the cupboards, and scribbled a long grocery list on a paper napkin. My stomach whined as I pictured Russell and the girls waking up to the smell of coffee and the perky sound of bacon sizzling. They would walk into the kitchen and find me standing in a patch of bright sunlight, scrambling some fluffy yellow eggs accompanied by a stack of golden brown toast—not Delphine's usual burnt offerings. Their faces would light up and they would beg me to stay forever. Looking at my shopping list, I remembered going to a twenty-four-hour market once with Delphine in the middle of the night to get some eardrops for Bonnie. Russell's car keys were sitting in a cut-glass candy dish on the counter next to a clutter of coupons and bills.

Once outside, I momentarily lost my nerve. Russell's bedroom was next to the driveway. I stood there for a moment weighing the risks—waking Russell versus running out of gas in my Nova—and then remembered how Delphine always used to brag that Russell could sleep through a tidal wave. Besides, just this once, I felt like driving the T-bird. There was no traffic this time of night. What harm could it do? I climbed in quietly, rolled down the windows, and let the car roll backward toward the street. At the end of the driveway, I turned the key and sailed off in the general direction of the highway.

The night had cooled some. The wind brushing my face revived me and I drove fast, over the speed limit, even though normally I am a slow and timid driver. Still—force of habit—I was slowing to a halt for a yellow light up ahead when some external force suddenly wrestled my foot down hard on the accelerator, laughing as we sped through the intersection. I recognized the laugh. Delphine the Speed Queen. Both Delphine and Earl always drove like bats out of hell, not a cautious bone in their bodies. Needless to say, they hit it off like long lost soul mates at our wedding. They were both reckless, uninhibited dancers. When we got the wedding pictures back, I burst into tears. There were more shots of Earl and Delphine than of Earl and me. Earl called the photographer and raised hell. Just past the Tastee Freez on the right up ahead I was relieved to catch sight of a blinking neon sign—NITE OWL MARKET. WE NEVER SLEEP.

There were only two other cars in the parking lot—a shiny Cadillac and a dilapidated pickup. I swung in carefully next to the Cadillac, leaving as much space as possible between the T-bird and the old truck, as if rust and dents were contagious. Inside, after the humid velvety darkness, the market seemed too bright and too cold. Squinting and shivering, I pushed my cart up and down the aisles, tossing in bacon, eggs, oranges, milk, sweet-cream butter, cinnamon Danishes, a barbecued chicken, potato salad, and a large jar of French's mustard. The full cart, piled high with good food, filled me with a sense of well-being. Standing in the checkout line, I tore open a bag of peanut M & M's and popped them into my mouth, one by one, as I scanned the headlines on the scandal sheets. My favorite was BLIND MAN REGAINS SIGHT, DIVORCES WIFE. Ahead of me, a stylish black couple in evening clothes was buying champagne, Doritos, and spermicidal sponges. I piled my more mundane groceries on the counter.

"That comes to 28.68," the cashier announced brightly, as if I had just won something.

I returned the *National Enquirer* reluctantly to the rack, paid the cashier, hefted the two big bags—one in each arm—and walked back out into the warm dark night. The black couple was just driving off in the Cadillac. The old pickup looked lonesome, like an ugly wallflower standing there in the otherwise empty lot. That's when it hit me. The Thunderbird was gone. My intestines lurched. I broke out in an icy sweat. *Gone.* Russell's baby. I stood there blinking, staring at the space where I had left it, as if this were some sort of optical illusion. Some cruel magic trick. Then I stumbled back through the automatic door, dropped my bags on the counter, and wailed, "Call the police. My car's been stolen."

The cashier stopped smacking her gum and perked up. She buzzed the manager, who materialized from the back of the store and led me swiftly to his cubbyhole, attempting unsuccessfully to calm me down. While he was dialing the police, patting my hand and smiling reassuringly at me, all I could think about was how Russell was never going to speak to me again. Not one word. And I thought what a terrible thing it was for him to lose Delphine like that and then me—so to speak—not a week later, like this. Not to mention his car. And then it suddenly dawned on me how he didn't *have* to know, at least not about my part. Not ever. For all he knew, the car could just as easily have been stolen right out of his own driveway. And, at that instant, it was as if I'd accidentally floored some internal accelerator pedal. My arm shot across the desktop, slammed down the button on the telephone, and motioned for the manager to hang up.

"Never mind," I said. "There is no car."

The manager looked bewildered, as if he were waiting for the punch line.

"This is terribly embarrassing." I extracted a Kleenex from my purse and blotted the perspiration from my neck and brow. "I just now remembered my son dropped me off here on his way to work. He works the night shift at, at—" I sighed and shook my head. "It's this new medication. For my heart." I fanned myself with the Kleenex and shut my eyes. "Half the time I don't know whether I'm coming or going." I blinked back the tears, which were real enough. "I can't tell you how silly I feel."

The manager smiled, obviously relieved. No police. No bad publicity.

"Just call me a taxi, if you'd be so kind," I said. "I'll wait outside on the bench. I've been trouble enough already."

The taxi driver was young and friendly and foreign and seemed eager to practice his English. One half of my brain carried on a polite Conversational English dialogue about the weather while the other half rehearsed what it would say when Russell discovered the T-bird was missing. Sitting there in the taxi cab, staring at my reflection in the dark window, I practiced an expression of blank shock.

"You can stop right here." I pointed to a house a couple of doors down from Russell's. The cab screeched to a stop. I handed him a ten-dollar bill and got out with my groceries. "Thank you and have a nice night," I enunciated slowly and carefully. "You are welcome. The nights in Florida are very balmy," he said as he sped off.

My heart was pounding, fearful that Russell might have woken up while I was gone, but the house was mercifully still and silent. Breathing a little easier, I tiptoed into the kitchen, fished Russell's car keys out of my purse and set them back in the candy dish. A minute later, as I was unpacking the groceries, I picked the keys up again and wiped my fingerprints off with a paper napkin. Once the food was all put away, I turned out the kitchen light. Barefoot, I tiptoed down the hall to Delphine's sewing room and lay down on the narrow daybed. I slept fitfully. Several times during the night I awoke with my heart hammering like a judge's gavel and had to remind myself that I, in fact, was not the thief. The real thief was probably sound asleep, snoring like a baby. Lying there wide awake in the dark, I suddenly remembered I was hungry. In the early morning quiet, I could hear the M & M's rolling around like loose ball bearings in my empty stomach.

At seven A.M., after my short sleepless night, I was already frying up the bacon when the girls wandered into the kitchen in their matching flowered babydolls. They didn't seem particularly surprised to see me there. I chatted up a storm while Noelle gulped her fresh-squeezed juice and Bonnie heaped raspberry jam on her toast. I was jumpy, bumping into things and losing track of sentences halfway through, but the girls were too busy bickering with each other to notice. In the back of the house, I heard the shower clunk off, and my stomach muscles jackknifed as I slid some picture-perfect eggs onto Noelle's plate. "Yick," Bonnie wrinkled her nose and pretended to gag.

"Well hey. What's all this?" I was standing at the stove, my back to the doorway, when I heard Russell's voice. He sounded cheerier, more like his old self.

"Good morning, Russell." I turned and smiled. His wet hair was neatly combed and he was wearing a fresh polo shirt the color of the T-bird.

"I'm starved." He sat down at the head of the table and grabbed a Danish.

"Sleep well?" My hands trembled as I spooned the rest of the eggs onto his plate.

"Like a baby." He dug right into them, eating nonstop as the girls, taking advantage of their new tragic status as motherless children, wheedled for various indulgences—a new pair of Reeboks, money for the movies, a ride to the mall. At the word *ride,* my heart nearly threw a rod. I concentrated on washing up some dishes at the sink. The girls went to their room to change into school clothes. I blasted the water in the sink, and Russell continued to eat in silence. After a couple minutes, he thanked me for the breakfast and said he thought he might as well go to work for a few hours, ease back into it. I just nodded, my back to him. He sighed and picked up his keys from the candy dish. "You know, I still can't believe she's really gone," he said as he headed toward the front door and closed it gently behind him.

I went on running the water in the sink, rewashing the same plate over and over, holding my breath. A second later, just as I knew it would, the door crashed open again and he stormed back into the kitchen, white-faced underneath his deep tan, breathing heavily, muttering curses. He didn't say a word to me. It was as if I weren't even there. And I didn't say a word to him. Not even when he yanked the receiver off the wall phone next to the sink, practically strangling me with the cord, as he dialed the police.

After they had all finally left—the police, then the girls, then Russell—I collapsed at the kitchen table. We'd all told the police the same thing: we were asleep and had not heard a sound. The two officers looked a little bored by it all and did not seem to find anything amiss, or even unusual. They acted as if *not* having your car stolen were unusual. Although the younger black officer's eyes did light up some when Russell showed him the color snapshot of the Thunderbird. He whistled and looked a trifle more sympathetic as he handed the picture back to Russell. The older one with the basset hound eyes said the car would probably wind up in Miami with a new paint job. At the word *paint*, Russell smacked his fist into his palm and let out a low moan. "My wife died last week," he said. "And now this."

Both officers mumbled their condolences and glanced my way as if Russell were talking about *me*, as if maybe, in all the furor over the stolen car, they had overlooked the fact I was dead.

"I'm his sister-in-law," I said. "I stayed to help out with my nieces."

They nodded and looked relieved. As they trooped out, the basset hound said what surprised him was that the car had not been stolen years ago, as if Russell had been driving around on borrowed time. This made me feel a little less guilty. It seemed it had been bound to happen sooner or later, one way or another. Once the police were gone, I handed Russell the keys to my Nova and a twenty for gas. "Go to the club," I said. "Work will take your mind off it." I held the screen door open for him. He hesitated for a moment—like a reluctant cat—and then walked outside. As I watched him cross the street to my car, I felt a warm surge of relief. *I had gotten away with it.* Followed by an abrupt splash of cold fear. *Now what?*

My stomach growled, a deep and menacing sound in the empty quiet of the bright kitchen. Delphine had left the kitchen nice and neat, which surprised me. She was never much for housework. It was almost as if she'd been expecting me. The white linoleum sparkled in the morning sunlight. The stainless steel gleamed like a mirror. I felt light-headed, woozy. Almost twenty-four hours—it seemed like years—since my last meal. I craved sweetness. My hands trembled at the memory of yesterday's Black Forest cake. I stood up shakily. It seemed to me that I had never known such hunger. But when I opened the refrigerator, Delphine's refrigerator, and looked at all that good food I'd bought—cinnamon rolls, barbecued chicken, potato salad—I realized that I had long ago bypassed the hun-

ger point, and now there was nothing I wanted to eat, nothing
I could eat. There was nothing that could satisfy my hunger. It
felt like some fairy-tale curse, an evil spell. I saw myself standing there forever, growing thinner and thinner, shivering in
the refrigerated air, starving. I forced myself to peel off a sticky
white-frosted Danish, but as I raised it to my lips, I felt a wave
of nausea and quickly tossed it, like a Frisbee, back onto the
foil tray.

After a minute, maybe longer, I shut the refrigerator door
and sat down again at the kitchen table. My hands were still
trembling and my stomach was grinding its gears like an old
car with a bad transmission. Glancing idly around the room,
my eye lighted on the snapshot lying face down on the floor
where it must have blown off the table. I bent over and picked
it up. A younger Russell was standing in the driveway, hosing
down the T-bird. He was smiling flirtatiously at someone.
Probably Delphine. Earl used to smile at me that way sometimes. I turned the picture over and anchored it with a saltshaker. When Earl died, after I'd found that strip of photos, I'd
been too hurt and too angry to grieve for him properly, but all
of a sudden, the pain was just as sharp and bright as some un-
used wedding gift, a set of steak knives hidden away in the
back of the closet all these years. Poor Earl. No matter what
his sins, he'd more than paid for them. I started to cry, then
stopped abruptly as it occurred to me that maybe Earl and
Delphine were together somewhere, some otherworld disco,
dancing up a storm. Even dead, Delphine was probably more
of a live wire than I ever was. But for the first time, I didn't
begrudge her. Or him. I can't say I liked the idea, but it would
be a crying shame for all that energy to go to waste. After the
dancing, they'd have worked up an appetite, and Earl would
probably take her out for Chinese, one of those dim sum
joints, and the waiter would lose track trying to count up the
stacks and stacks of little saucers, like so many poker chips, on
Delphine's side of the table.

I turned the snapshot face up again, half-hoping to see Delphine's greedy, generous smile reflected in the gleaming hood of the car, but there was nothing there. Just sun shining on sky-blue metal so clean you could eat off it. As I studied the picture, my stomach rumbled again, loud and impatient, and out of the blue I remembered something, something I had read in the newspaper years and years ago about some man who had eaten a car, a whole car, bit by bit. It had been some sort of a bet or maybe a dare. At the time I remember thinking the man was crazy. Maybe he was. But suddenly I felt I knew why he'd done it, I knew what sort of hunger had driven him to it. And I knew that if I were to walk outside and see the Thunderbird sitting there in the driveway, glazed by the afternoon sun, I would start eating, and I would not stop until there was nothing left to steal.

Camelot

When I wake up again, the bedroom is an indeterminate gray—it could be dawn or dusk. The bed is littered with used pink tissues like so many wilted roses on a parade float. I have been dreaming, I have a fever. A copy of *Swann's Way* lies open on the tangled bedclothes. I have been dreaming in rusty French. I have been dreaming about Sondra and Arthur. The gray is San Francisco, the fog. In my dream there was the strong aroma of garlic and leeks. I reach for one of the crumpled tissues and blow my nose. My nose can't smell anything, but the scent of the garlic and leeks lingers inside my fogged brain. According to the clock, it is dusk. At the foot of the bed, the television is on, the sound off. Footage of JFK—on the campaign trail, on a sailboat with Jackie, in the Oval Office, Dallas. Jackie in her pink suit and pillbox. For the past two days, floating in and out of consciousness, doped up on antihistamines, I have seen the same footage over and over. The shots are as familiar to me as snapshots in my own family albums, more familiar. It is the twenty-fifth anniversary of the assassination. The TV is full of Kennedy. In my drugged and feverish state, this disorients me. A time warp. Sondra and Arthur and I eating *escargot*. At first I am repulsed, but then I start to like them. At any rate I like the idea of myself eating them: now you have eaten *escargot*. It was always like that when I was with them—as if I were re-membering it all as it was happening. A slight time delay. As if it were all being beamed to me by satellite from across the ocean.

This was 1963, the year I graduated from college, the year I left home. I had grown up in a small town in western Washing-ton state and attended the local branch of the state university, living at home with my parents and two younger brothers, ma-joring in French and working part-time in the library, reading Balzac and Flaubert and George Sand. My favorite book at that time was *Bonjour Tristesse*. There were not many French lit majors at Western Washington State—I had been inspired by our foreign exchange student, Brigitte, in high school—and

Professor Lemaire took a special interest in me, lending me her own dog-eared copies of Marguerite Duras and Anaïs Nin. Once in a while she even invited me to accompany her to Seattle to see a French film—Renoir, Truffaut, Godard. Fortunately for me, her husband did not like subtitles. During the long drives, she would chat to me about her childhood in Paris, referring to specific streets and cafés as if I were of course familiar with them, even though she knew that I had never set foot out of the United States. Our conversations would be conducted in French. I had an uncanny, inexplicable talent for the language, as if I had been French in some previous incarnation. I was hopeless in German and only passable in Spanish. I was like one of those idiot savants. My parents thought I was crazy, wasting my time. But I didn't care. Dr. Lemaire was my champion; she believed in me. In my senior year she pulled some strings—the daughter of a close friend was an assistant professor in the Modern Languages Department at San Francisco State—and I was awarded a graduate assistantship. As a bon voyage gift, Dr. Lemaire presented me with an Edith Piaf album and a tiny flask of Bal de Versailles.

San Francisco, with its steep hills and rainbow Victorians, seemed as exotic and sophisticated as Europe. It was just before the whole hippie era transformed the city, before Haight-Ashbury and love-ins in Golden Gate Park. I rented a small room in a large apartment within walking distance to campus. My roommates were three other female graduate students— two in English and one in art history. Of the three, I was the only one who had never been to France and the only one who actually spoke French. They thought I was something of an oddity—like a deaf person majoring in music theory. A few years later, when I finally got to Paris with my husband on our way back from India, I felt let down; it had loomed too large in my imagination for too long. The usual complaints—food was expensive, the people were rude, it drizzled every day. I envied my colleagues in the dead languages who could never visit Sparta or Gaul. I was just as glad I had dropped out of graduate school.

But in the summer of 1963 it was a different story. I was walking around campus humming *La Vie en Rose* wrapped in a cloud of Bal de Versailles like a stray dog looking for a kind master. And I found one in Dr. Mignon—or Sondra, as she insisted I call her—Dr. Lemaire's friend and my boss. I was her research assistant, starting that spring. I had never called any of my professors by their first name and although it thrilled me, it also initially embarrassed and unnerved me. Those first couple of weeks I avoided addressing her by name and even when I left her notes, as I frequently did, asking her some factual question, I left off the salutation. Looking back, I can see that she was really quite young still herself—not even thirty—but at the time—I was twenty-one—she seemed impossibly sophisticated and mature. She had been to Vassar and the Sorbonne. She had been married, briefly, to a French journalist and amicably divorced. She wore chic but messy Parisian clothes—a hem sagging, a button missing—and her abundant dark hair was artfully pinned up in such a way that you held your breath waiting for it to tumble down. She wore narrow black sunglasses even on those days when the sun was tucked behind a dense blanket of fog. She made risqué puns in Franglais. She smoked Gauloises.

My first task as Sondra's research assistant was to index her just-completed book on Madame de Staël. Sitting in a windowless cubbyhole adjacent to Sondra's office, I worked day and night, checking and cross-checking, my desk piled high with hundreds and hundreds of index cards. (This was before computers hit the humanities.) Sondra was off for the summer and only showed up at the office infrequently—to rummage through her surprisingly neat files for something or to meet a colleague for lunch. To me she was always pleasant on the run. Once, on the spur of the moment, seeing me hunched over a stack of index cards, she invited me to join her for coffee at the student union, where she quizzed me girlishly about my romantic—or rather, sex—life. Since then I have met other women with this same talent for instant intimacy, but Sondra was my first. In the space of twenty minutes I told her all about Tommy Hubbard, my college beau, and the fact that I had allowed him to relieve me of my virginity as a sort of going-away gift from me to him. Sondra smoked her Gauloises and nodded her approval—I think she had been afraid I was still a virgin. For the first time, she offered me a cigarette. I took it and puffed on it, afraid to inhale.

Suddenly she looked at her watch. *"Merde!* I told Arthur I'd meet him at the DeJonge at two. Do you know Arthur?" She leapt up and plunked a couple of dollars on the table. "Art Schiffman? The poet? Teaches a couple of courses on French poetry in translation."

I shook my head. "I've heard his name."

"Well, you'll have to meet him," she said. "You'll like him. Maybe lunch at my place next week?"

I nodded casually, too thrilled to speak, and she took off in such a rush she left her dark glasses sitting on the table. I slipped them on and wore them for the rest of the afternoon.

The following Friday I finished the index two weeks ahead of our projected schedule and called Sondra to tell her it was done, *fini.* She sounded even more delighted with me than I had fantasized. *"Tu es un ange!"* she exclaimed. I demurred. In the background I could hear commotion and music. "Just a minute," she said, holding her hand over the mouthpiece. I could hear a low masculine murmur. Palms sweating, I berated myself for clumsily interrupting them in bed. Then she laughed, taking her hand off the mouthpiece, and said, "Listen. I'm just giving Arthur a cooking lesson. Leek soup and *escargot.* Why don't you come over? We've got enough food for Napoleon's army."

"Well, I don't know, if you really . . ." I stammered feebly, waiting to be convinced.

"Take a cab," she interrupted authoritatively—"we'll be waiting"—and gave me the address on Telegraph Hill.

All the way there in the cab I wished I'd had time to run home and change out of my jeans and shabby black sweater into some chic yet unassuming and incredibly flattering little number that I didn't actually own. But when I arrived at Sondra's apartment, I was pleasantly surprised to see that both Sondra and Art were wearing jeans and sweaters as well. I felt blessed that I'd not had enough time to follow my own stupid instincts. Even now, after twenty-five years, one of my worst nightmares is to arrive somewhere overdressed. Sondra kissed me on both cheeks, European-style, and led me by the hand into the kitchen, where Art was busy slicing mushrooms paper-thin with the delicate concentration of a neurosurgeon.

"Art, this is Nancy Long, my miraculous research assistant from heaven." Sondra reached up and rearranged the pins in her tumbling hair, then handed me a measuring cup full of egg yolks. "Here. Whisk these," she said.

I stared uncertainly at the gaudy yolks. Grilled cheese sandwiches were about as far as my culinary expertise extended.

"You do know how to whisk, don't you?" Art said in a husky, vampy voice.

Sondra groaned. I looked blank.

"Don't tell me you've never seen *To Have and Have Not?*" he asked me. I shook my head. "Where did you say you're from?" He sliced the last mushroom and swung his sandaled feet up onto the kitchen table.

"Bellingham, Washington." (Actually I was from Nooksack.)

"Well, that explains it."

"Don't mind him," Sondra said. "He thinks anyone who grew up west of Brooklyn is a savage." She knocked his feet off the table and handed him a head of garlic. "Shut up and mince."

Art smiled at me and winked. "These French chefs are so imperious." He was short and slight with closely cropped black curls and horn-rimmed glasses. Except for his mouth, which was rather feminine and sensitive, he did not look at all like my idea of a poet. (A couple of years later, browsing in a London bookshop, I came across a new book of his—*Songs of Innocence and Guilt*—and in the jacket photo he was wearing rimless glasses, his hair cascading lyrically to his shoulders.)

At a loss for small talk, I was standing slightly apart, facing the window which had a spectacular view of the bay. The sun was sparkling on the water. Sondra and Art were bantering back and forth in the most witty and sophisticated manner about what an impossible tyrant she was, and the aroma of mushrooms sautéing in butter, garlic, and wine was wafting through the kitchen. Cool European-sounding jazz was on the stereo, like background music in some subtle, bittersweet foreign film. And that was the first time I remember having the odd sensation that I was not really there, present in the moment, so intent was I upon fixing every small detail in my memory. I had that transient feeling, the tourist's hunger to record and preserve. At the same time as I was struggling so hard to appear cool and nonchalant, I wanted desperately to whip out my camera and take snapshots.

"Here." Sondra took the whisked yolks and handed me the cookbook. "You read me the directions aloud." She pointed to the recipe for Escargot Façon du Chef. The directions were in French. I hesitated, suddenly nervous. In Washington state my French accent was a marvel, but perhaps it would sound less marvelous in San Francisco. Art was watching me with the bemused, amused expression I soon learned was characteristic of him. The ash from his cigarette toppled into the bowl of strawberries he was rinsing.

"I've been trying to think who she looks like," he said to Sondra. "Jeanne Moreau. A blond Jeanne Moreau, don't you think? The eyes and mouth."

Sondra squinted at me thoughtfully for a moment and nodded, probably more—I later realized—out of a courteous desire not to contradict Art (or Arthur, as she called him) than any sincere agreement, but at the time it was just the boost I needed. I cleared my throat and launched into a dramatic reading of Escargot Façon du Chef, rolling my *R*s and generally hamming it up in such an exaggerated fashion that they were both doubled over, gasping for breath; Sondra's tears were plinking into the simmering sauce; and I had never been quite so pleased with myself—and perhaps never will be again—as I was at that moment.

Lunch was a long, lingering affair with much wine and hilarity. I was relieved and emboldened to discover that intellectuals, professors, could act so silly and talk such lighthearted nonsense. At first I pushed my snails around on my plate, panicked and sickened at the thought of actually putting one in my mouth, but, luckily, a couple of glasses of wine in quick succession served to suppress my provincial squeamishness. After the first tentative bite, I was surprised and elated to discover that they were not in the least slimy. Art was in charge of the wine. As soon as a glass was empty, he would reach over and refill it. "Nature abhors a vacuum," he'd say. When we'd drained the first bottle, he leapt up and deftly opened a second. He seemed to know his way around Sondra's kitchen, and I naturally assumed that the two of them were "an item," until, about halfway through lunch, Art made a passing reference to someone named Janice, and I said, "Who's Janice?"

"My wife," Art said, as if it were no big deal, and the conversation sailed on smoothly. Stunned, I surreptitiously studied Sondra, looking for some sign of distress, but she seemed completely unperturbed. My own reaction, however, was not lost upon Sondra—nothing ever was—and when Art excused himself to go to the bathroom, Sondra patted my hand reassuringly. "Arthur and I are just good friends," she said. I nodded quickly, worried that she would think me too conventional and stodgy. "I think we'll all be good friends," she said, leaning back and lighting a Gauloise. "Don't you?"

I nodded again. My brain was fuzzed from all the wine—I

wasn't used to drinking in the afternoon—and I felt close to tears, on the verge of making some embarrassingly maudlin remark, when Art reappeared with the bowl of strawberries in one hand and carton of sour cream in the other.

"I love it when my friends all get along," Sondra sighed contentedly and bit into a strawberry.

"What makes you think we're getting along?" Art said, perfectly straight-faced.

After dessert, Art and I started clearing the table, but Sondra gestured impatiently for us to stop. "Just leave it," she said. "There's something I want to show you." She hurried off toward the back of the apartment. Art flipped over the record on the stereo. I sat down rather primly on the chrome-and-leather sofa, the only piece of furniture in the room other than the floor-to-ceiling bookshelves. The room suggested someone with expensive taste and little money, unwilling to make compromises. Art sprawled on the other end of the sofa, lit a Camel, and fiddled with the venetian blinds so as to soften the glare. Squinting out the window, I could feel my brain bobbing buoyantly inside my head like the small white sailboats dotting the bay. Alone suddenly with Art, I felt a little nervous, girlish. I had not had that much experience with men except for Tommy, whom I had known since the fifth grade. We'd gone to the same orthodontist. I didn't think of Tommy so much as a man as a full-grown boy; he was not in the least bit "other." Art got up and came back with a bottle of cognac and three snifters just as Sondra reappeared, hugging a large glossy book to her chest. Her face was flushed, as if she'd been bending over searching for the book, and her hair was even more disheveled than usual. In her crimson sweater she reminded me of an overblown rose.

"This is the book on *châteaux* I promised to show you, Arthur." She sank down on the leather sofa between us and opened the book on her lap. "Arthur and Janice are planning to rent a house in France next summer," she explained to me, smiling serenely—look, Ma, no jealousy. Sitting so close to her, I caught a whiff of Joy, my favorite perfume that I never failed to spray myself with whenever I passed through a department store. Thousands of distilled rose petals. Fifty dollars an ounce. She turned a page. "A friend of my parents rented a smaller estate near this one a few years ago, near Tours. Their son and I had an affair. Every afternoon between four and five. I was supposed to be tutoring him in French. Instead we were screwing our brains out." She laughed. "His parents paid me four dollars an hour."

"And how was his French?" Art asked.

"His oral skills were excellent." She winked at me. I blushed and gulped my cognac.

"Tsk, tsk." Art leaned back and covered my ears with his hands. "You're corrupting her. Behold, she blushes."

"She's not so innocent as she looks," Sondra said. She smiled her confidante's smile. "Tell him about Tommy."

"Yes, tell him about Tommy. By all means," Art said. "I'm all ears."

"He's no one," I mumbled. "I mean, he's just someone back in Washington."

"Waiting for you?" Art splashed some more cognac in my glass.

"I guess so. He wants to get married—he wants *us* to get married and join the Peace Corps." I accidentally sloshed some cognac on my lap and rubbed it into my jeans. "He's studying mechanical engineering."

"And how about you? What do you want to do?" Art coaxed.

"I don't know," I shrugged. "Get my Ph.D. Be a French professor somewhere."

"Like Sondra here?"

I nodded. "Exactly like Sondra." I sounded so drunkenly earnest they both burst out laughing.

"We haven't found you a *château* yet," Sondra said, suddenly brisk, like a teacher steering a wayward class back on track. "How about this one? Château Villandry." She turned the page to an imposing stone castle complete with moat and mazelike formal garden.

"I don't know," Art mused. "Do you have anything a little more with-it? Maybe a split-level with a wet bar?"

The three of us sat there sated from the rich meal, sipping our brandy and joking about the pros and cons of the various *châteaux* with a kind of timeless, dazed concentration that blanked out the rest of the world. As if the apartment were surrounded by a deep wide moat. Finally Sondra closed the book and stretched, letting her head fall back against the sofa and her eyelids flutter shut. The book slid off her lap with a solemn clunk. Like obedient children, Art and I also sank back and shut our eyes—I opened my left eye just a crack to make certain that his were indeed closed. It reminded me of naptime after story hour at my kindergarten, when we would all curl up like so many little shrimp on our blankets. I was smiling, about to comment on this, when I felt Sondra's hand on my leg, lightly stroking the inside of my thigh. My muscles tensed involuntarily, a quiver of pure shock. For a split second she paused, her fingers acknowledging my sudden tension, and then continued. Just as involuntarily my muscles relaxed themselves again. I cracked my eye open wide enough to observe that Sondra's other hand was similarly stroking Art's thigh. This is weird, I said to myself, but my mental voice sounded distant and hollow. You should make some excuse and leave, the voice said, but I ignored it. Here in this room, with the quiet jazz and the sun reflecting off the bay, the voice seemed as remote and out of place as my mother's scolding me to get my elbows off the table. Sondra's fingers were flirting and playful, kittenish. I shivered in the warm sunlight. On the other end of the sofa I heard Art moan softly, dreamily. There must have been a clumsy sort of transition from sofa to bed, but I cannot remember one. In my memory it is all as fluid and natural as flowing lava, or some deftly edited foreign film. In one frame we are sitting on the sofa fully clothed and in the next—

voilà!—we are lying on the bed, our naked bodies softly lit, needing no direction from anyone, every gesture a brilliant ad lib, a virtual masterpiece of erotic improvisation.

In the sudden quiet aftermath of the sensual explosion, that awkward moment when awkwardness returns, when you fall back into your separate selves, Sondra stretched luxuriously, lit a Gauloise, exhaled, and said, "I do so love it when my friends get along."

We nearly, as my teenage sons used to say, busted a gut laughing. I dared to reach over and flick a tiny speck of tobacco from the corner of Sondra's lip.

A few hours later, back in my little rented bedroom unable to fall asleep, I had an attack of guilt about the way I had more or less dismissed Tommy in conversation—not to mention what came later. In the middle of the night, I sat down and wrote him a long chatty letter about nothing. At the end, after only a slight hesitation, I lied and said that I missed him.

That was mid-June. For the next few months, the three of us met at Sondra's apartment usually once a week for our "French cooking lessons." I did in fact, among other things, learn to make Coq au vin, Coquilles St. Jacques, ratatouille, an excellent cheese soufflé, and bittersweet chocolate mousse. It was a shame that my husband was your basic steak-and-potatoes man. I probably could have made some other man with a more sophisticated palate very happy.

There was a Fourth of July barbecue at Art and Janice's. Sondra was away, visiting her current love, who was living in London for a year on a Fulbright. My roommates were also throwing a big bash in our scruffy little backyard, something I had actually been looking forward to—I had recently vowed to spend more time with people my own age—but I was too curious to turn down Art's invitation. I had never met Art's wife. In fact, I had never really seen Art without Sondra. The curious thing about this whole thing—or one of them—was that it was always the three of us together. I can, of course, vouch for the fact that Sondra and I never made love alone, never even spent much time alone together. And Sondra maintained that she and Arthur had never gone to bed without me—a claim that I believe, strange as it all may sound. The three of us seemed to form an equilateral triangle, some perfectly harmonious triad. At the time I was too naive to realize just how rare this was. A small-town girl at heart, I sometimes brooded over the dubious moral nature of our little *ménage à trois*, but I more or less took its success for granted.

"Just bring some beer," Art had said on the telephone. "We're having burgers. Nothing fancy." Still, Janice had obviously gone to quite a bit of trouble making homemade potato salad, cole slaw, and brownies. She was a short, bosomy woman—the kind who wears loose flannel shirts and painter's pants—sisterly, maternal—the sort of woman who grew up with lots of brothers. I liked her immediately and immediately felt at home, even though I recognized only one other person, a grad student in comp lit. Sitting in a webbed lawn chair watching Art flip hamburgers on the grill with his twin daughters, Aviva and Ariel, clinging adoringly to his pants legs, I marveled at this double life of his, and in the midst of such wholesome and attractive domesticity, I experienced another swift attack of guilt and remorse. How unhealthy and sordid those long gourmand afternoons in Sondra's darkened bedroom seemed suddenly in comparison to all this daylight and fresh air and simple American food.

When I got home that evening, I called Tommy long-distance. At first he was cool, still miffed that I had rebuffed his offer to drive down for the long weekend, pleading too much work, but gradually he warmed up, never any good at holding a grudge. He was all excited. He had gone to talk to some Peace Corps volunteers just returned from West Africa. The volunteers had shown slides and talked about what a great experience it was. They had even met President Kennedy at a White House reception. (Tommy's and my romance had blossomed the summer we both worked as eager young volunteers at the

Kennedy campaign headquarters in Bellingham.) Yes, I said, it did sound wonderful. I even promised to give it some serious thought. "You know, you sound more like your old self," Tommy said. But the following Tuesday I was back at Sondra's apartment for another cooking lesson.

A few weeks later, the fall semester started. I had enrolled in Sondra's graduate seminar in Proust on Wednesday afternoons. At the first class meeting, I took my seat at the seminar table among the dozen other graduate students in a state of smug, exalted agitation. I had imagined there would be an undercurrent running between Sondra and me, significant glances in my direction, veiled innuendos. In essence, I would know myself to have been singled out, chosen, promoted from the ranks of the other fawning grad students. But as Sondra waxed eloquent about the possible influences of Bergson, Schopenhauer, and Kierkegaard on Proust, it became more and more impossible for me to imagine her naked, her articulate tongue educating me in a completely different mode, and I began to feel like some pathetic and delusional creature. Wounded by her perfectly blank eyes devoid of any faint flicker of recognition, I had to fight my childish urge to betray her with my own telling look or remark. As the hour progressed, I grew more dejected and paranoid, interpreting much of what Sondra said as an oblique personal rebuke. I scribbled down one quote from a critic that struck me as particularly pointed: "Marcel yearns after a kind of mystical communion, with an individual, or with a group, dwelling, he believes, in a superior realm of existence separated from the vulgar herd." Distraught as I was, I should have remained silent, but something kept compelling me to speak up, and my comments or maybe my tone must have seemed a little off. I noticed some of my classmates eyeing me skeptically. Then, during the ten-minute break, Sondra called me into her office on some pretext and shut the door. "What goes on out there is purely professional. Don't take it so personally." She kissed me swiftly on both cheeks.

"Comprends?" I nodded, delighted and ashamed of myself. After that, I was fine. Really, that's all it took. She was my teacher. I learned.

Things continued much the same all through the fall. I was busy with my studies. I socialized some with my fellow grad students in French lit. I talked to Tommy long-distance at least once a week. And, of course, there were the French cooking lessons. The weeks passed quickly. Suddenly, it seemed, it was late November. I was flying home for Thanksgiving. I was not exactly looking forward to it. I was, in fact, half-dreading this reunion with what now seemed to me to be some former life, some alias. All summer and fall I had made excuses. I had diplomatically but successfully managed to avoid seeing Tommy, to avoid making any decision, but there was no excuse possible this time. Our connection seemed to stretch thinner with every passing week, but I was still, for whatever reason, reluctant to sever it. Plus, my parents were anxious for me to be there. The family had always been together at Thanksgiving. Sondra and her Fulbright lover were meeting for a week's holiday in New York. Art and Janice and the twins were driving to her parents' house in Scottsdale. It was a hectic time, but we managed to schedule one final pre-Thanksgiving cooking lesson—a brunch this time because Sondra had an appointment to get her hair trimmed that afternoon—Friday, the day before we would all scatter in our various directions—Friday, November 22, 1963.

I got up early that morning in order to give myself plenty of time to pack before taking the bus to Telegraph Hill. It was cool and damp and quiet. Peaceful. My roommates had already left for home. I had always enjoyed packing—the geometric precision of it—and I had traveled so little that the mere sight of a suitcase still produced a childlike thrill. We were supposed to meet at Sondra's at ten o'clock. Sondra would make coffee. Art would pick up some croissants. I snapped my old Samsonite shut and straightened up my room, wanting everything to be neat and orderly upon my return.

For some reason, Art, who was notoriously late for everything, was early this particular morning. He was just hunting
for a parking place in his battered MG as I got off the bus. We
walked down the block and up the stairs together, chatting
about nothing in particular. Art's hair was still damp from the
shower—little, dark ringlets—and he was carrying a white
paper bag from the bakery. The croissants smelled fresh and
buttery. Suddenly I was starved. Sondra opened the door still
in her red silk kimono—no pretenses here, I remember thinking. The aroma of French roast filled the apartment. A newspaper was lying on the doorstep. I bent down and handed it to
Sondra. She tossed it onto a pile of unread papers on the
kitchen counter. The kitchen clock, shaped like a coffee pot,
said 10:02. (Just past noon in Dallas.) Sondra poured us coffee
and arranged the croissants on a pretty stoneware platter.

We drifted into the living room. The phone rang. Art and I
sat on the sofa, drinking and eating, while Sondra tried to cut
short the conversation with whoever it was on the other end. It
was a gray day outside—or maybe that's just how I see it in
retrospect. Art reached over and brushed some flaky crumbs
off my sweater. His hand on my breasts aroused me. There was
something urgent and hurried in the atmosphere that morning—we all felt it—none of our usual languid postponement
of pleasure. Sondra hung up and then, on second thought, left
the receiver off the hook. We followed her into the bedroom.
She had not even bothered to make the bed or change the
pink flowered sheets from the last time. As she slipped off her
robe and stretched out on the bed, I thought she seemed a
little sad or depressed. I thought possibly she might have quar-
reled with Paul, her London paramour, but then again she may
have just been tired. I was tired myself, having stayed up till
one A.M. reading a scholarly essay on Proust that Sondra had
recommended entitled "The Inhuman World of Pleasure." Sitting on the edge of the bed, I made some lame little joke about
the title as I reached my arms back to unhook my bra—a
black-lace extravagance I had invested in after our first cook-

ing lesson—(a year or so later we would all abandon bras)—
and Art said, "That's good. Don't move." I turned my neck
slightly and was startled to see him standing there naked,
focusing the lens of an expensive-looking camera. Instinctively
my hands flew to my bare breasts and I looked at Sondra, waiting for her to protest. She was reclining, one pale arm flung
wantonly over her head, like one of Matisse's *odalisques*,
smoking the butt-end of a Gauloise she'd fished out of the
overflowing ashtray beside the bed. She just smiled and gave a
Gallic sort of shrug. Slowly I let my hands fall away from my
breasts. Sondra bent over and kissed, one by one, the bony
vertebrae of my spine. With my eyes closed I could still see the
camera flashes, little stars of light in the darkened room. I
thought I might die of pleasure.

It was just past eleven when we left. Sondra's hair appointment was for eleven-thirty in Union Square at a place called
Rapunzel's—funny the things you remember. She was showering when Art and I took off. He offered to give me a ride home,
and even though it was out of his way, I accepted. A fellow grad
student was driving me to the airport at one-fifteen. Conversation was fitful and a little strained. I think we both felt a bit
embarrassed—like two strangers emerging from a matinée of
some porno film, blinking in the sudden dazzle of daylight. We
were both tired, physically spent. As if in sympathy with our
mood, the streets seemed oddly empty and subdued. Art lit a
cigarette and said, "I should have a radio put in this heap." He
drummed his fingers along the steering wheel. I kept thinking
I would be at home by dinnertime. Sitting in the dining room
eating my mother's pot roast. It seemed impossible.

When I walked up the steps to my apartment, the phone was
ringing. I heard it ringing as I fumbled the keys out of my big
purse, and it kept ringing as I flung open the door and raced
for the kitchen. I was afraid maybe it was my ride to the airport
calling to say her car had broken down or something had
come up. Skidding across the linoleum, I grabbed the receiver
off the wall and gasped a breathless hello.

"Where the hell have you been?" he burst out, then paused as if to collect himself. It was Tommy, but his voice sounded weird, choked. He was supposed to be meeting me at the Seattle airport, and my first thought was that he was calling to say he was sick.

"What's up?" I said, immediately launching into a long-winded, guilt-ridden excuse about where I'd been. He cut me off.

"Don't you *know*?" he said, incredulous. "Didn't you *hear*?" His voice was loud, and it suddenly dawned on me he was crying. I had never heard him cry before. My heart froze in my chest.

"What is it? What happened?"

"It's Kennedy," he said. "He's dead. He was shot and he's dead." His voice rose at the end of the sentence, as if he were not *telling* me but *asking* me something of grave importance. What flashed into my mind, oddly enough, was an image of Sondra sitting in the beauty parlor.

I caught the plane to Seattle on schedule and spent the weekend with Tommy and my family, glued to the television set, watching the president's funeral. Thanksgiving afternoon, Tommy and I went for a long drive along the coast. We held hands in the car. We didn't talk much—we never had really— but I felt closer to him. Before he had always seemed confident and competent, but now I was seeing a new, more vulnerable side of him. Kennedy had been his hero. We stopped for a beer at some roadside bar, and Tommy's eyes filled with tears as he was sitting there, not saying anything. I wanted to comfort him. I covered his hands with mine and squeezed hard. He blew his nose with a paper napkin and then excused himself for a minute. When he got back from the men's room, I could see he had splashed cold water on his face and combed his hair—pulled himself together. He ordered two more beers and then, when the waitress had gone, he asked me to marry him and join the Peace Corps. He said they were looking for people to go to India. He said if I didn't go with him, he would go without me. Outside it was pouring rain. I pictured hot dusty countryside, emaciated oxen, dark-eyed children, flies, simple meals of rice and chapatis, ascetic pallets. Long days, hard work. Ask not what your country can do for you. "Okay," I said. "Let's do it."

I never even went back to San Francisco to pick up my belongings. I was afraid. Pleading a family crisis, I asked my roommates to pack up my books and clothes and ship them up to Bellingham. Tommy offered to drive me down there to get my things, but I said no, and he did not press the issue. I think he sensed I had my reasons, reasons he was better off not knowing anything about. The thought of seeing Sondra and Art again made me feel sick. It was like aversion therapy. When I thought of being in bed with them, I would close my eyes and see Jackie in her pink suit and blood-stained nylons, that look of pure anguish on her face. By way of explanation of a sort, I sent Sondra a postcard on which I had copied out a quotation from *Remembrance of Things Past* that I'd remembered reading in "The Inhuman World of Pleasure," that essay which Sondra had so highly recommended:

> The duke felt a momentary alarm. He could see the delights of the ball snatched away from him . . . now that he had been told of the death of M. d'Osmond. But he quickly recovered and flung at his two cousins a retort in which he declared, along with his determination not to forego his pleasure, his inability to assimilate the niceties of the French language: "He is dead! Surely not, it's an exaggeration, an exaggeration."

Tommy and I had a simple ceremony—close family and a few friends—low-key and subdued. After all, we all still felt as if we were in mourning. In January we left for Bangladesh, where we lived for two years. After India, we traveled for six months and then moved to Chicago, where Tommy got a job with the city—some urban development agency—and I went back to school to get a master's in elementary education, specializing in reading skills. For a few years I taught elementary school. Then I moved on to spearhead a task force on literacy. We had two sons, both of whom are away at college now. After the younger one, Rob, left for Stanford, Tommy and I divorced. Not so amicably.

I live alone and work only part-time now as a consultant on literacy programs. For the first time in twenty years, I find myself with free time on my hands. Too much time. A few weeks ago, in September, I enrolled in an adult education course on Proust taught by a retired professor emeritus from the University of Chicago. The course is taught in translation, which is just as well, because my French is so rusty. Still, my professor seems impressed by my background.

It is dark now. I am feeling a little more human, my head is clearer. The rubble of crumpled Kleenex offends my sense of order. I reach for the wastebasket, eyes glued to the silent television screen as the camera zooms in on Jackie in her black veil. Haunting. Unforgettable. A cultural touchstone. Idle cocktail-party chat. Where were *you* when Kennedy was shot? And each time, newly caught off guard, I experience the same sudden flush of shame and desire as I mumble my little lie: in the language lab, I say, listening to French tapes.

From time to time over the years, I would think of those photographs that Art took that last morning—I would picture them in my mind, shot by shot—and hope to hell that he had the good sense to burn them. But now suddenly I hope that he was foolhardy enough to lock them away somewhere safe— our own private little footnote to history. Sighing, I retrieve my copy of *Swann's Way*, which has tumbled onto the floor. Dressed in a little double-breasted coat, John-John salutes his father's casket. God. Has it really been twenty-five years already?

The Zealous Mourner

"You're alive," David said, "that's the main thing. That's all that really matters."

"Your wife is disfigured, your only wife has only one breast. Doesn't that matter to you?"

"Of course it *matters* . . ." David paused, confused. "But it's not the *main* thing. There are degrees of tragedy. I can live with this."

"Well, that makes one of us," Louise said, snapping off the light.

"Christ," he sighed into the darkness. "You'd think you were Jayne Mansfield, some airhead bimbo, not an intelligent, successful professional woman. I married you because I—"

"Jayne Mansfield was decapitated," she interrupted. "That must be the worst." Louise's hand flew to the empty place on her chest. It felt to her fingers like a crater, although she knew it was just flat. Since the operation, she had spent considerable mental time weighing the relative gravity of various possible disfigurements and impairments: the loss of an eye versus the loss of a leg, arm, voice, hearing. One day she had even dug up an old insurance policy and studied the cash awards—fifty thousand for an eye, ten thousand for an arm, no mention of breasts.

"You'd think you'd been decapitated. You should be glad you've got brains, interests. You're a *tenured professor*, for chrissakes. When's the last time—"

"Just *shut up*," she shouted. "Please."

"All right." He rolled over, his back to her, and yanked the blanket over to his side. "But I really think you should call Alice," he said for the hundredth time. "Good-night."

"Good-night." She kissed the back of his neck, a guilt kiss. "Maybe I'll call Alice in the morning," she lied.

Alice was her therapist. She had helped Louise through some rocky times, but Louise had no desire to talk about this particular affliction with Alice or any other therapist. The mind, the spirit, who cared? It was her *body*, her perfect body with all

103

its flaws, she wanted back. She was tired of the mind, hers and everyone else's. She thought maybe if she had it all to do over again she'd become a tennis star, or at the very least an aerobics instructor. And maybe she'd stay married to Teddy Flynn. Which was another good reason to steer clear of Alice. Alice would make her talk about Teddy, try to analyze the dreams. Since the operation, she had started dreaming about her ex-husband for the first time in years. They were only married for two years, twenty years ago, and she'd only married him because her mother had died of cancer that spring and she was all alone. No father (he had died years earlier). No sister, no brother. Alone. Although at the time, of course, that's not how she saw it. At the time it was all hot summer evenings and clandestine skinny-dipping and sad songs on the car radio and aftershave that smelled manly—like someone strong and capable of taking care of you forever—and the scratch of stubble against her cheek, the taste of rum and Coca-Cola, his lips nuzzling her breasts like candy.

The Teddy dreams were erotic and at the same time a little sad, as if mournful, romantic music were playing in the background, and Louise did not want them analyzed, reduced to archetype, by Alice or anyone else. She just wanted to keep dreaming them.

In his sleep David hunkered against her backside and draped a heavy arm over her waist. His hand sleepwalked up her belly toward her chest until she intercepted it and slid it back down—like a teenage virgin, only in reverse. In those days the trick was to keep their hands *above* the waist. The boys were like babies you had to distract from danger with bright, shiny objects. Whenever one seemed too intent upon tugging off her underpants, she would pop a breast out of her bra and wave it around beguilingly until his attention shifted safely upward. With Teddy Flynn it was different. She never had to resort to such maneuvers. From a family of flat-chested women, fresh from Vietnam and a series of R & R flings with small-boned Asian bar girls, he'd seemed stunned, dazed, by the sight of her generous American breasts. Night after night, parked on some dark lovers' lane even though she lived alone in an empty house full of empty beds, he paid such court to her mammary glands that she began to feel like a mermaid. Eventually her neglected lower half began to thrash and demand its share of attention until they finally did IT, and she decided THIS MUST BE LOVE.

Two years later she'd decided THIS COULDN'T BE LOVE. How odd, she'd thought: it had taken her two days to work up the courage to marry him and two years to work up the courage to divorce him. She couldn't believe how much harder it was to say "I don't" than "I do." The day she finally left him, he stood at the front door watching her get in her car, the same car he'd sold her two years earlier. He reminded her of a dog—a big, sad, obedient dog that someone parks on the curb and orders, "Stay!" For a long time after that she didn't much like herself. When she told her life story to new friends and lovers, she edited out the part about having been married. She took the snapshots of her and Teddy out of her photo albums and hid them. She hadn't even told David about her brief first marriage until after she'd moved in with him and he'd stumbled across the snapshots of Teddy while searching through the closet for the heating pad.

"Who are they?" he'd said, staring at a picture of Teddy and her cutting the wedding cake, as if he expected her to tell him she had an identical twin sister she'd neglected to mention.

"A *used-car salesman*," he'd laughed when she told him. "Come on. I know you're kidding."

Suddenly she had a need to see those pictures again. The digital dial blinked 3:15, but she didn't care. She didn't have to wake up early any more. She had extended her semester's leave of absence indefinitely even though everyone, *everyone*, had told her that was exactly what she should *not* do if she wanted to get back on track, back to her old self. Her old self minus a breast, that is. No one mentioned that. Except the trickle of volunteers, women with one or both breasts missing, women who had been in her shoes and who came to talk to her like a special maimed branch of the Welcome Wagon. One woman sat on the edge of Louise's hospital bed, holding her hand and talking earnestly about the miracle of survival. Every thirty seconds or so she would squeeze Louise's hand hard, as if pumping something into her. Another woman, who visited her at home one afternoon, yanked the bedclothes off and asked Louise just who she thought she was to lie around feeling so sorry for herself when she had a nice home and husband and fancy job?—giving Louise the distinct impression that this woman, a double mastectomee, had none of the above. Yet another woman, younger and more glamorous, came with tiny twin daughters dressed in identical pink bathing suits, like animated Valentines. They were on their way to the beach, she'd explained, a strategy calculated to show Louise that the good life goes on. As she was leaving, she'd pulled down the strap of her black tank suit and exhibited her breast to Louise. "Reconstructed," she'd said. "Not bad, do you think?" She'd asked Louise if she wanted to feel it and Louise had said no, although she did. "A lot of the Hollywood stars go to him. He has a special back entrance his nurse showed me." One of the pink twins wet her pants and the woman departed hastily, slipping the plastic surgeon's card in the mailbox on her way out. That night Louise made fun of the woman to David. They were eating take-out Chinese food and he was laughing, nervously pleased that she seemed to be regaining her sense of humor, when she'd stopped suddenly and shivered. "I used to be a nice person," she said. "Didn't I?"

"Of course, of course you were. Are." Tears sprang to his eyes and he had reached for her, and she had held him at bay with a chopstick. It left a fiery dot of sweet and sour sauce on the snowy breast of his white shirt. He'd stormed out to the kitchen, muttering to himself. A second later he'd loomed in the doorway, sponge in hand, and said, "If you don't call Alice right now, I'm going to call her for you. And drive you to the appointment myself."

She continued eating her rice.

"Well, what do you have to say to that?" he'd demanded, anxiously biting his cuticle—a habit she had broken him of back in graduate school.

"You can lead a horse to water but you can't make her drink."

"God!" he'd pounded his fist against the door frame. "God, you piss me off!"

"I'm sorry." She had finished her rice and moved on to what was left of his.

"And I have news for you." He waited for her to look up at him. "You were *never* all that nice."

"I was too."

"Oh yeah? What about Tommy Flynn? Why don't you ask that poor schmuck just how nice you were?" He marched over and grabbed the telephone receiver and brandished it until he felt foolish and set it down again in its cradle.

"Maybe I just will, as a matter of fact," she said. "I've been having these dreams about him lately. Pleasant dreams. *Very* pleasant dreams. And his name is *Teddy*, as in bear."

David was a sound sleeper. He had two modes—on and off. She always felt the instant he woke up. It was like a furnace kicking on in the basement. She could hear his mind rumbling beside hers on the pillow. Conversely, when he was asleep, there was nothing—she doubted that even a brain scan would pick up any activity. She slid out from under his arm, quietly closed the bedroom door, and turned on the hall light. The two photo albums were buried under a heap of racquets—tennis, badminton, squash, racquetball. She carried an album into the bathroom, locked the door, sat down on the toilet lid, and flipped through the slightly sticky pages, passing by snapshots of college, of a summer trip to England, Scotland, and Wales (with her mother), and of her small candy-colored wedding—everyone managing to look simultaneously stiff and

wilted in their best clothes in the ninety-five-degree heat—
hurriedly flipping the pages until she was at Lake Tahoe with
Teddy on their honeymoon.

They had arrived in the late afternoon, unpacked—she had
insisted on unpacking his suitcase in a fit of wifely domesticity—and made love before dinner. She remembered his
being miffed by all her giggling every time his empty stomach
grumbled. In between giggling fits she murmured apologetic
reassurances. Passion spent, they showered and dressed and
debated restaurants—Italian, Chinese, steak, and seafood. She
was straining, arms akimbo behind her back, to hook her black
bra when he reached over and said, "Let me." She let her arms
hang loosely at her sides, enjoying this classic bit of married
life, when he suddenly slid the bra off and tossed it onto the
bathroom floor where it skidded into a puddle.

"You don't need that," he said. "It's 1966. California. The
natural look."

"But—"

"Do it for me. Your loving husband. Please."

She had looked at their image in the mirror, like some
multiarmed Indian deity. He was standing behind her, his
hands caressing her unbound breasts with such a sweet, con-
tented expression on his face.

"Okay, I guess," she'd giggled.

He kissed the back of her neck.

They went to an Italian place on the highway and she remembered holding the large red menu over her breasts while
they gave the waiter their order. She also remembered driving
back to the hotel with her legs squeezed tight, her bladder pain-
fully full, because she had been too self-conscious to saunter
all the way back to the ladies' room with her breasts bobbing
like buoys beneath her thin summer dress. But by the end of
the week she was playing volleyball on the shore and parading
around in skimpy T-shirts, bestowing breezy, oblivious smiles
on the oglers as Teddy puffed with pride of ownership.

There was one snapshot she particularly liked. They were standing in front of the yellow Mustang, the car he'd sold her. The car door was open and you could almost hear the radio playing. A sliver of blue lake floated in the background and Teddy's arms cinched her waist, swinging her round and round. His tanned, muscled arms were pushing her breasts up, and they threatened to spill over the top of her strapless sundress like foam over the rim of a glass.

She slid the snapshot out from behind the cloudy plastic page. As her fingertips traced the pneumatic curve of her glossy breasts, she could hear her mother's patient voice telling her not to touch the image, to hold the picture by the edges—like so—and suddenly, more than anything, she wished her mother were asleep in the next room, wished she could see her mother for one minute, wished she could feel her soft hands, hear her cluck of sympathy. But her mother was dead, of cancer, and Louise was alive. Lucky to be alive. That's what everyone kept telling her, and she didn't get it because she never for one second thought she was going to die. Louise had watched her mother on her sickbed and had come to the conclusion that no one ever really believes they're going to die until they're already dead, and then it's too late to worry. What it's not too late to worry about is everything just short of death.

"What're you doing?" David cleared his throat, scratched his groin, and squinted into the bright bathroom. "At this hour."

"Nothing. I couldn't sleep." She hastily jammed the picture back into the album and feigned a yawn. He reached for the album and shook it until the loose picture fluttered out. She stomped on it with her bare foot, but it slid easily out from under her toes.

He glanced at it and sighed. "I have to pee." He handed the picture back to her. "If you'd be so kind."

She stood up and he raised the toilet seat, careful not to brush against her. She remembered the orange-robed monk she had accidentally bumped into on the crowded ferry in Bangkok, the horrified look in his eyes as she smiled apologetically and reached out her arm to steady him. Later she read in a guidebook that the monks were forbidden to touch females and that the Thai women scrupulously gave them wide berth. She was in her strident feminist phase back then and had gone wild when she read that.

"From now on every monk I see I'm going to pat his ass."

"No, you're not," David said calmly. "It's a cultural difference and we respect cultural differences."

She'd stuck her tongue out at him and he'd patted her ass, and she'd socked him in the gut and they'd ended up rolling around on the bed, an hour of athletic sex that left them lying sweaty and exhausted, contentedly immobile, on top of a pile of crinkled maps and train schedules.

They had not made love now in over four months, since right before the operation. Her fault. He could not have behaved more heroically, showering her with flowers, champagne, lacy negligees, compliments, protestations of love. Yet she'd thought he protested too much. Such romantic fuss was not like him. They had been colleagues before lovers. Their marriage had flourished in the glow of reading lamps, not candlelight, and although they had always enjoyed each other in bed, the fact that they were of the opposite sex had always seemed like more of a boon than a necessity. So it made no sense to her now that the loss of a single breast could cause this rift between them. But it had.

On her way out of the bathroom she hit the light switch, then paused in the semidark to admire him naked for a moment, one of those alabaster gods peeing in a Roman birdbath.

"You should have an affair," she said.

"Don't tell me what to do. You're not my mother."

She laughed. He could still make her laugh. That was something at least.

He flushed the toilet. "What makes you so sure that I haven't, that I'm not?" He followed her down the hall to the bedroom.

"Because I know you."

"And what is it you know?" He waited until she was settled back in bed and then climbed in delicately on the other side.

"I know you couldn't stand thinking of yourself as the sort of unenlightened schmuck who cheats on his wife after her mastectomy."

"You don't give me much credit." He rolled over, his back to her.

For the first time it occurred to her that maybe there actually was someone else, another woman who listened sympathetically while he confided to her the details of his dismal home life. The thought of this other woman judging her filled Louise with white-hot indignation. Who was *she* to judge *her* until she had walked in Louise's shoes? Then it suddenly occurred to her that it would be just like David to find someone who *had* walked in her shoes, just to make her look bad, to leave her no room for argument. She imagined David lying in bed with the glamorous blond with the reconstructed breast, the two matching little Valentine girls sound asleep, innocently sucking their identical thumbs, in the next room.

"Don't blame yourself, Dave," she'd stroke his mussed hair and whisper into his ear. "You've done everything anyone could do. It's her. It's just her. She's a sick woman, Dave."

"But I'm her husband," he'd protest. "I'm an intelligent, sensitive man, not some macho jerk. I should be able to help."

"Some women just don't want to heal, Dave. They're like emotional hemophiliacs. They'll bleed all over you if you give them half a chance." She'd slide her hand under the covers until she found what she was looking for, and he'd bestir himself to show his gratitude.

Gratitude. She remembered this odd habit of Teddy's. He used to thank her after they made love. Every time without fail, he would kiss one breast and say "thank" and the other breast and say "you." It got on her nerves after a while, and finally she blew up and screamed, "For chrissakes don't thank me! It's not like I'm doing you some big favor." He got that wounded-deer look in his eyes and said, "Okay. I'm sorry." After that he stopped thanking her aloud, but she could tell he was still thinking it, and the silence was louder than the spoken words.

"What did you *see* in him?" David asked her once. "I don't get it." He was staring at one of those Polaroid Christmas cards that Teddy had sent her. The color picture on the card showed a paunchier Teddy with his new wife, Lorraine, and their ten-month-old baby, Brian Jeffrey. The card had arrived out of the blue six years after their divorce and represented the sum total of their communication over the years.

While she was busy chopping an onion, David affixed the card to the refrigerator with a sushi magnet and printed at the bottom, "Would you buy a used car from this man?"

"You're a disgusting snob," she'd said when she'd turned around and noticed it finally. "And if you want to know the truth, I'd trust him over you any day." She'd snatched the picture off the refrigerator and slid it into her pocket, then resumed mincing the onion with a new threat of violence. "He was the sweetest, gentlest, most selfless person I've ever known. Absolutely no ego. No personal ambition. Not like our kind. A kind of latter-day saint, really." Her eyes were tearing, her nose sniffling. "Needless to say I didn't appreciate him at the time. I didn't think he was smart enough for me. One afternoon we went down to the Motor Vehicle Department to take our written driving tests together. I got 100 percent and he flunked. When I saw that big red *F*, I felt humiliated. I felt contempt. And that's when I knew for sure I was going to leave him. Over a stupid grade on a stupid driving test. And the irony was, he was the best driver in the world, the very best." She wiped her eyes, then blew her nose in a paper towel. She knew she sounded like some maudlin drunk. David stared at her amazed, not quite daring to laugh.

At dawn she was still awake, watching the darkness fade to gray, listening to the birds' clatter. She feigned sleep while

David showered and dressed and foraged in the kitchen. As soon as the front door shut behind him, she fell asleep. When she woke up, she was alone and smiling. The smile faded along with whatever she was dreaming, leaving only a vague afterimage of Teddy and a vast parking lot full of toy cars, like a parking lot glimpsed from an airplane. It was late. The bed was ablaze with sunlight, and she was sweating in her flannel night-gown. As she peeled the nightgown off over her head, her naked body exuded the odor of old coffee grounds. She threw on the sweatpants and sweatshirt that she had worn the day before and probably the day before that. Then she walked out to the kitchen, poured herself some coffee, and sat. She had no plans for the day. There was nothing she had to or wanted to do. She looked lazily at the hand-painted calendar hanging on the wall opposite her, a gift from a former student, and saw that in some former lifetime she had drawn a line through the first three days of this week and scrawled in the title of a con-ference at UCLA she had planned to attend. For an instant she could remember, relive, sitting here in the kitchen, skimming the brochure, and hastily penciling in the dates on her calen-dar. For an instant she was possessed by the spirit, the spirit of her former busy, confident self. It was as if some dervish had lifted her up, whirled her around, and then dropped her back to earth, stunned and winded.

Louise suddenly felt an ache in her left breast, the one that wasn't there. She frequently felt some sensation there. She knew it was a common phenomenon—the phantom limb. Everyone had heard about amputees who could still feel their missing arms and legs. She had read about one man, a Vietnam vet with his leg amputated at the thigh, who kept waking up at night to scratch the sole of his missing foot. The itch even-tually drove him insane. This reminded her of an off-the-wall joke she'd heard on Johnny Carson: my girlfriend has poison ivy of the brain—the only way she can scratch is to think of sandpaper.

The summer she married Teddy she had picked some wild-flowers and come down with the ugliest case of poison ivy ever. Her fingers blistered and swelled like sausages. Three times a day Teddy would patiently swab her hands with Calomine lotion and then tenderly position a cottonball between each of her fingers to keep them from chafing against each other. She sat there in the rocker on the front porch like some splay-fingered queen of Sheba, restless and whiny, while he cooked the dinner and washed the dishes, whistling away just as cheerful as could be. It was after dark by the time he joined her out on the porch. She was complaining about the itching when suddenly he leaned over and unbuttoned her blouse and parted it like a curtain so he could look at her bare breasts. "Are you *crazy*? Button it," she hissed at him. She clawed clumsily at the front of her blouse, her fingers too swollen to maneuver the tiny mother-of-pearl buttons. Neighbors were passing by on their evening constitutionals, and although her chair was angled facing the house, she was sure they could see. "Lovely evening!" he called out. "Just enjoying the view." He smiled and winked at her. She frowned and muttered at first, but pretty soon she was aroused, so aroused she wouldn't have murmured a peep of protest if he'd stripped her naked right there on the front porch in full view of passersby. They let it build like that for just as long as they could withstand the heat, then tore inside and went at it like a house afire.

Afterward he lay quietly with his head on her breasts humming that song "Louise." Then they took a long hot shower together. Every now and then he'd hold one of her breasts to his lips like a microphone and warble some silly song until she slapped his hand away. She used to sigh and wonder if all men carried on like such fools. She found it hard to imagine Jean-Paul Sartre, for instance, clowning around with Simone de Beauvoir's tits. She fantasized having silent, sophisticated, high-brow sex with pale, bespectacled men. Years later, one of the things that most attracted her to David was his dignity in bed.

That and the fact that he seemed virtually indifferent to her large breasts.

So how—the thought cracked like a whip in her brain—could she now expect him to grasp the enormity of the loss? She had chosen him for his very lack of fanaticism, and now suddenly she wanted him to mourn like a true zealot. It wasn't his fault. He was simply miscast. The right man for the wrong job. It was perfectly obvious.

She leapt up from the table, suddenly energized, and hurried into the bathroom. Moving quickly and mechanically, she showered and dressed and packed a small suitcase. On the way through the kitchen to the garage, she scribbled a hasty note to her husband—

Back in a couple days. Don't worry.
It's not your fault. Love you.

—and stuck it on the refrigerator with the sushi magnet.

It was after midnight, raining lightly, when she took the Petaluma Boulevard South exit off of 101. Her shoulders and lower back ached from the nine straight hours of freeway driving, but other than that the trip was a blur, as if she'd been suspended in a trance. A trance that had not yet worn off. It was too late to call him this evening, she knew, yet she continued down Petaluma Boulevard, away from the strip of highway motels, and turned left onto D Street. Even though she had not heard from him in over a decade, she knew in her bones he would still be living in the same house, and in fact, as she pulled up to the curb and looked across the street at the one lighted window on the second floor—their old bedroom, her mother's old bedroom—she saw him stand up, look out at the street for a moment almost as if he sensed something, and then shut the window. As simple as that. She was so tired she could barely keep her eyes open as she headed back out to the highway, back to the lonely little strip of motels.

The next morning she was jostled out of a deep, dreamless sleep by voices in the next room. For an instant she thought she was back in the hospital, but then she heard a car door slam right outside her window and she remembered. She got up and dressed, dressing more carefully than she had in some time. She arranged her dark hair so as to hide the gray streaks and put on lipstick, then wiped it off. She wanted to look as much like she had back then as possible, and back then she had not worn makeup. She left her things in the motel room and drove to some bright, anonymous place on the highway for coffee. Although she'd had nine straight hours alone in the car to think, she didn't have much of a plan really. She felt as if she were obeying some more powerful will than her own. She sat there calmly, drinking her coffee, waiting for some voice from the wilderness to tell her what to do next. Go ye forth and . . . The waitress brought her the bill.

It was a cool, sunny day, crisp as new money. Perfect car-selling weather. Teddy had always said you had to work twice as hard to sell a car in the rain. She headed out toward McBride Buick and Olds on the west end of town. Although it seemed almost inconceivable that anyone could work in the same place for twenty years—she thought of her address book, crossed out and written over as her friends moved on to better jobs, bigger houses—it seemed entirely possible that Teddy had stayed put, had remained loyal to Walter McBride. When she arrived at the corner where the car lot used to be, her heart sank. There was a minimall with a donut shop, auto parts, 60 Minute Photo, and a deli—all catty-corner to a huge new Toyota dealership. She parked and went into the auto parts store, looked around for the oldest clerk, and asked him whether McBride Motors still existed.

"Oh sure," he said. "They're out on the highway now. Practically in Novato." He drew her a little map.

He was such a nice man and her relief was so great to hear the place still existed that she grabbed the first recognizable

item she saw—a pair of sunglasses—and said, "I'll take these."
She didn't realize they were mirrored until she glanced in
the donut shop window on the way back to her car and was
startled to see herself.

The map was precise and detailed, and she found the new
location without any trouble. McBride Motors was twice its
former size but still only half the size of the new Toyota place.
She drove over toward the service area and parked incon-
spicuously, as if waiting for someone. She kept her new sunglasses on. A couple of young salesmen were out on the lot
talking animatedly with prospective customers. She felt conspicuous and unpatriotic in her silver Saab. Except for the
anachronistic cars, she could have been in some time warp.
She was beginning to feel like Peggy Sue in that Francis Ford
Coppola movie, filmed right here in Petaluma, in fact, about an
unhappily married woman who gets conked on the head at
her high school reunion and winds up back at Petaluma High.
The trance was beginning to wear thin around the edges. She
was thinking about getting the hell out of there when the voice
in the wilderness said, "Wait!" She paused with her hand on
the ignition key, and then she saw him. He was wearing a suit
and talking with two younger salesmen. It was evident from
the younger men's demeanor that he was their boss. This surprised her. Somehow she had never thought of Teddy climbing the success ladder along with everyone else. He looked,
actually, thinner and more fit than in the Christmas picture he
had sent her years ago.

A mechanic walked over, wiping his hands on a greasy
rag, and asked her if she needed help. "No," she smiled in-
gratiatingly, "I'm just waiting for a friend." When she looked
back over at the sales office, Teddy and one of the younger
salesmen were climbing into a shiny red car. Lunchtime, she
supposed. She noticed the mechanic glancing back over his
shoulder at her suspiciously. She supposed she couldn't very
well hope to sit here all day without attracting attention. It was

now or never. She could telephone, wait until he came back from lunch and then call, but she thought some physical proof of her presence, her nearness, was necessary. She took one of her cards from her wallet and was about to scribble a note on the back when she thought no. The card said "Dr. Louise Jensen" and would only serve to remind him of all the time that had passed and all the differences between them. She tossed the card on the floor and tore off a large white scrap from a McDonald's bag.

> Dear Teddy,
> I'm here in Petaluma. I drove up here just to see you. Please meet me at the Buckhorn when you get off, around 5? 6? I'll wait. I won't leave til you get there, so please come.
> Louise

She thought about giving him the name of her motel, where he could leave a message, but she did not want to make it easy for him not to come. Better he should think of her sitting alone at the Buckhorn waiting. She walked over to the young sales-man who was left, handed him the folded note, and asked him if he would please give the note to Mr. Flynn. "It's very im-portant," she said as she turned to go. "Business. You won't forget?"

"Right. I'll see to it personally." He made a big show of tuck-ing the note carefully in his wallet.

She could tell by the way he watched her get back into her car just what sort of business he thought it was. Well that was stupid, she thought as she drove away. Small town like this. He was probably the wife's kid brother.

At a quarter to five she was sitting in a booth at the Buckhorn nursing a draft beer. She disliked beer, but she figured that Teddy would order one and she didn't like the image of her-self sipping white wine while he chugged on a beer. The after-noon was a blur. It would take a shot of sodium Pentothal to make her remember how she'd managed to while away the past four and a half hours since leaving the car lot. Her brain revved and idled as she waited. Her hands and feet felt like ice, but she was sweating underneath her chamois shirt and bulky tweed jacket, which she kept buttoned as if he could walk right in, take one look at her, and tell what had happened, what was missing. The Man with X-ray Eyes. One of the two loud, beefy men at the bar was giving her the bold eye. She frowned down at her beer and got some morbid, vengeful pleasure out of imagining letting him coax her into bed and the look of horrified shock on his beer-bloated face as his hand groped under her sweater.

At 5:30 she ordered a second beer. It did not occur to her to wonder what she would do if he didn't show, because she knew he would. It was just a matter of when, when he could get away. Then an awful thought occurred to her: what if he didn't come alone? What if he brought along one of the young salesmen or, worse yet, his wife? Teddy was the above-board, open-book type. He didn't know the meaning of the word intrigue. She got up and went to the ladies' room—the beer seemed to pass straight through her—and when she walked back out to the main room, there he was, standing uncertainly at the front of the bar, alone. He stiffened when he saw her, and she suddenly wondered what she was doing there. Four hundred miles from home. An image of the pay phone hanging next to the ladies' room flashed in her brain, and she fought a quick urge to run back there and dial David or Alice and have them talk her back home, the way air controllers sometimes talk lost pilots safely back to earth.

Teddy followed her back to her booth.

"Thanks for coming," she said.

"I was surprised, you know, out of the blue like that. How long's it been?" He took a sip of his wine. "Almost twenty years. I recognized the handwriting, though, right away." He paused for a long minute, nervously fingering his tie, waiting for her to explain herself.

"Give me a minute," she said. She downed the rest of her

beer and signaled the waitress for another. She wasn't half drunk enough.

"So," he frowned. "You look good, real good."

"Come on. I look like hell." She started in on the new beer. Her hands were shaking and she sloshed some on the table.

"No, not at all. A little tired maybe," he conceded, blotting the spilled beer with his napkin. "You were always hard on yourself."

"And on you."

He shrugged. "I'm married now. Again."

"You mean since Lorraine?"

"No. I mean Lorraine. Fourteen years. How did you know her name?" He looked a little paranoid, as if he suddenly suspected her of something.

"Christmas card one year."

"Oh." He smiled, relieved. "We have two kids. Brian and Amy."

God, she groaned to herself, waiting for him to pull out the wallet and the pictures. For this she drove four hundred miles. She reached across the table and grasped his hand to prevent him from reaching for the wallet. Embarrassed, he glanced over at the bar for a moment, then slipped his hand out from under hers. She started to cry quietly.

He sat there looking at her, seemingly paralyzed by cross impulses. She could imagine the battle going on in his soul: the impulse to be loyal to his wife on the one hand, the impulse to give comfort on the other.

"Come back to my motel room with me," she whispered, staring down at her hands now folded primly in her lap. "Please. Just this once." She pressed her leg against his under the table. "I need you to."

Automatically he moved his leg away, then let it drift slowly toward hers again, just barely touching. "I don't know what to say," he said. "I'm happily married. I thought you were married." Suddenly a light seemed to dawn. "That's it, isn't it? You're getting a divorce."

She shook her head. "David's fine."

"Oh. Good." He seemed deflated, overtaxed, at a loss. He finished off his wine and glanced at his watch. "Lorraine will be worried. I'm sorry." He started to reach in his pocket for his wallet, this time to pay. He put enough bills on the table to cover her, too.

"Thanks," she mumbled.

"I'm sorry," he said again. "I am."

He stood up and self-consciously struggled into his raincoat. "Look. Would you like to come over for dinner? I could call Lorraine and say, well, she . . ."

"No. No thank you. That's very sweet, though."

He shrugged and looked relieved but still hesitant to walk off and leave her like this—alone, in a bar, crying into her beer.

"Could you give me a lift to my motel?" she asked suddenly. "If you're not too late already."

"Sure. No problem." He seemed overjoyed to be given a concrete way to help. "How'd you get here?"

"Cab," she lied, as she followed him out to the parking lot past her Saab and got into the shiny red car she'd seen earlier in the day.

He turned on the radio and they didn't say much during the short ride to her motel. He attempted some chitchat about how Petaluma was changing—skyrocketing property values, gourmet restaurants, etc.—but when she didn't respond, he fell silent. She was sunk inside herself, straining to hear the voice in the wilderness, summoning her courage.

"Here." She pointed at a neon sign up ahead.

He swerved into the poorly lit, deserted parking lot, gravel flying.

"There." She pointed to a room on the end.

He coasted to a halt in front of her door. "Not exactly the Ritz," he joked. "I figured you'd be a millionaire by now. Or at least married to one."

"Do it now," the voice said. "Now."

"Come inside," she coaxed. "Just for a minute."

"No," he shook his head. "I can't. I'm sorry." He sighed and reached across her and opened the door.

"Please. I have to explain the way I'm acting. I have to show you." She started unbuttoning her jacket.

"Jesus," he groaned and rested his forehead against the steering wheel.

She finished the jacket and started in on her shirt buttons.

"Jesus *Christ*, what're you doing?" He scrambled out of the car and walked around to her side of the car. "You're crazy. I'm going to call your husband myself and tell him to come and get you 'cause you're just not yourself."

He held her jacket shut and half-dragged, half-carried her into the motel room, dropped her on the nearest twin bed, and then turned his back to her, fumbling in the dark to find the lamp switch.

"Shit, where is that fucking thing?" he cursed and muttered as he frisked the pole lamp.

It was comical, and she surprised herself by bursting into laughter. The light blinked on and he turned to glare at her, face flushed scarlet from exertion and exasperation. She stopped laughing and watched his expression change as he got a good look at her sitting there, stock-still, with her blouse gaping open. The color bleached out of his face, and he sank down on the edge of the twin bed opposite her.

"I've been dreaming about you," she said. "Ever since it happened. You were always so crazy about them. Treated them like pets."

"I used to drive you crazy. You used to threaten to handcuff me."

"Yeah. How the mighty have fallen." She caught a glimpse of herself in the large wall mirror and winced. "God." She buttoned a couple of buttons of her blouse and smoothed her wild hair. "I apologize. I have no right. I don't know what I'm doing really. I really don't know. I really don't. Last night I parked in front of your house. There was a light on upstairs in the bedroom, my mother's old bedroom. And all of a sudden I had this idea that I was your little girl asleep in my old room and you and my mother were about to go to sleep in her room, your room—our old room, yours and mine—and for a second I felt so safe. So comforted. For a second it all made sense, you know, like dream logic, and then it all fell apart. I don't know. I just don't know anything anymore. And now I can't seem to stop talking. I really can't." She paused for breath, hoping he'd say something. He didn't. She sighed. "You can go. You don't have to stay. I know she's waiting for—"

"Shhh. Be still." He sounded like a stern father.

"Sorry." She bowed her head meekly.

He leaned over and kissed her firmly on the lips as if to seal them shut, then rocked back and waited to see if she had anything else to say. She kept quiet. He smiled and knelt on the floor in front of her and unbuttoned her blouse.

"Beautiful," he whispered, "unique. The world's most perfect breast." He stroked her breast and gently pressed his lips to it.

"No." She shoved him away, wrenched her shirt free, and scrambled to button it. A button fell loose in her hand. She looked at it sadly for an instant, as if it were a tooth, then hurled it across the room. It nicked the mirror and bounced onto the carpet. "Shit!" Holding her blouse bunched together in the front, she crouched down on all fours and raked her fingers frantically through the red shag.

"Forget it. It doesn't matter." He grabbed her hands and wrestled her slowly down onto her back and pinned her there until her resistance snapped like a wishbone. Then, clumsily, he lowered himself down beside her and held her to him like a child, rocking her back and forth as if she were crying. But she wasn't. It was him. He was crying noisily, just as she had imagined he would be. A wonderful, terrible racket, more comforting than any lullaby. She closed her eyes and listened.

A Hole in the Language

I used to believe there is nothing new under the sun. Now what I believe is that there are no new words under the sun—except those having to do with computers—and that is the problem. People are suspicious of anyone or anything that can't be named. It's a sin against language, a sin against community. If you can't be labeled, you're like a car without a license plate—elusive and unaccountable, yet capable of doing great damage. That is the way they see you, and in fact, you do feel a bit out of control—at the same time tentative and reckless—as if all the street signs are in a foreign alphabet, and all you have to rely on are your own split-second instincts. Which is why Elka and I are so cautious now. We live our lives like drivers with our eyes glued to the flashing red light in the rearview mirror. We are braced for the siren's wail. We keep waiting to be punished.

Andrew, my ex-husband, has been as decent under the circumstances as anyone could be, but he is confused, almost dazed. "Do the two of you consider yourselves *married?*" he asks me, his voice, as always lately, straddling the fence between curiosity and animosity.

"We don't think about it," I say. "We're just . . . together."

Till death do us part, I think to myself. As it did us join. A fearful symmetry.

"Together," he repeats blankly, as if he has never heard the word before.

It is difficult to talk to him. His emotions are constantly turning inside out like a matador's cape. He wants to do "the right thing" but is not sure what that is, although everyone else seems to be. Well-meaning friends and relatives, including my own parents, keep urging him to sue me for custody of Grace, our eight-year-old daughter, whose anxiety manifests itself in odd ways. She has nightmares, and not long after Andrew moved out, I overheard her telling the postman that her father had been run over by a UPS truck, something that happened to our dachshund when she was five. She sees a child psychologist once a week—a precautionary measure.

Sometimes, lying in bed with Elka, I just do not know how all this came about, and I wish that Andrew and Grace and I had never moved to Denver, and that I had never met Elka. Not that I am not happy with Elka. Life with another woman seems so harmonious, so easy. I feel like someone who has lived abroad for many years and then suddenly rediscovers the simple, lazy joy of speaking in her native tongue. My hands and mouth have never been so articulate; my skin has never listened so attentively. Yet I fear that maybe I am just a small-town Midwestern girl at heart and I would be happier being unhappy than deviant.

Before Andrew, Grace, and I moved to Denver, we lived in Berkeley, where Andrew lives now. When he returned from London, alone, he rented an apartment on Panoramic Way with a view of Alcatraz. Grace visited him recently and reported that the place is so small he has no bed. There are wall-to-wall tatami mats, and when it was time for bed, the two of them unrolled their sleeping bags. They also ate exclusively with chopsticks. I imagine that Andrew enjoys this footloose opportunity to go Zen, and that defuses my guilt.

Our house was in the flatlands near the Oakland border— ramshackle and overfurnished. Andrew and Peter, his partner, built harpsichords in our garage, and I taught history at a private girls school in San Francisco. All the girls wore gray flannel blazers and knee socks and had pink-dyed streaks in their hair or asymmetrically shaved skulls that put me in mind of malignant brain tumors. They were so rich they seemed immune to life and cared nothing for history. I hated the job. In the mornings, Grace went to Montessori school, and in the afternoons, Andrew was around to keep an eye on her. It was through Grace's chatter that I finally, dim-wittedly, deduced that Andrew was having an affair with one of his customers—a prize-winning children's writer who lived in a restored Victorian in San Francisco and had commissioned an Italian virginal. When I asked him point-blank, Andrew admitted it was true and promised not to see her again. When the instrument was finished, his partner delivered it to the city. I hid the books she had given Grace, and Grace stopped mentioning her name. But occasionally the phone would ring and when I answered, the caller would hang up, and I always suspected it was she. During that split second of silence before the line went dead, I imagined I could hear our two hearts thumping in sync, our hands on the receivers connected by an elaborate circuit of electricity. I never ceased to hear her silence until we loaded up two U-hauls and moved to Denver the following summer.

In Denver I was completely happy for a month. We rented a pleasant house on the outskirts of the city. It had large sunny rooms and a small swimming pool, like a turquoise postage stamp from some Caribbean island. I had finally landed a job in my field: assistant professor of anthropology at Denver University. Andrew seemed busy and content, converting the garage into a workshop and making the rounds of the local music stores, establishing contacts. Grace made new friends quickly, inviting the neighbor kids over to swim, while her father or I played lifeguard in the ninety-plus-degree heat. Our next-door neighbors, Elka and Nigel Bentley, invited us to a Fourth of July barbecue to meet the neighbors. She was a weaver of some renown and he was a chemist for Bell Labs. Later that night, in bed, Andrew and I discussed the party, analyzed the other couples in that smugly superior way that couples have, and joked about investing in a riding lawn mower. I wrote witty notes to old friends in Berkeley about my fieldwork in the suburbs.

Andrew and I were getting along fine. We always did. The woman in San Francisco was all but forgotten. If anything, I was more curious than jealous. She represented a threat that had passed, a minor crisis swiftly dealt with. Andrew and I had grown up in the same small town, been together since our sophomore year at the University of Nebraska, could barely remember a time when we had not known one another. It was as if our past, our history, were some vital organ that we shared. It would take more than infidelity to blast us apart.

We kept meaning to invite Elka and Nigel to dinner, to return their invitation, but there never seemed to be enough time. I was busy preparing my classes for the fall, and Andrew was already working on a Flemish Double for a music professor at the university. Sometimes, in the afternoon, Elka and Max would come over. Max was only four, and Grace, who had just turned seven that spring, her maternal instincts in full bloom, hovered over him in the water. I liked to watch the tender way she strapped on his water wings and held his hand, usually against his will, as she escorted him into the house to go to the bathroom or get a cookie. However, like any mother, her patience would occasionally snap. More than once I had to yank her from the pool and send her to her room for clobbering Max with a kick-board. Elka just laughed good-naturedly and said, "He has to learn to fight his own battles."

Although he was small for his age, Max was fearless. Unfortunately, he seemed to have more courage than coordination and usually looked like a walking Band-Aid advertisement. Every few minutes, as Elka and I sat in lawn chairs or in the shallow end of the pool chatting away, I would see her start to call out to Max—"Slow down!" or "Watch out!"—and then force herself to let him be. She was thirty-nine when he was born, and she as much as admitted that she had only married Nigel because she wanted to have a baby. I assumed this was her subtle way of letting me know that she shared Andrew's and my assessment of Nigel as, at best, an odd duck and, at worst, a cold fish. He was a cartoonish cliché—the rational scientist with true British reserve—like Cary Grant in *Bringing up Baby*, only less humorous and handsome. But once she let me know the situation, Elka never complained about him, and, at least in our presence, she always treated him affectionately.

The last week in August, Andrew and I decided to take a week off before the semester started and visit my parents in Coral Gables. Elka volunteered to water the houseplants and take in our mail, and I told her that they should feel free to use our pool. The Sunday we left, I looked out our bedroom window as I was packing and saw Nigel floating in the deep end. He was sitting perfectly upright in a Styrofoam chaise lounge, wearing a Walkman (New Wave, Country Western?) and reading a book that even from a distance looked formidably technical. His nose was plastered with zinc oxide and he was wearing his rubber sandals. Andrew and I shook our heads and smiled.

We had a pleasant visit with my parents. Thinking back to previous visits, how we used to end up arguing and sulking over everything from U.S. immigration policy to red meat, it almost scared me to see how well we now seemed to get along without even trying. I asked Andrew if he thought it meant we were even straighter than we thought, that the suburbs were working their mysterious magic on us. He said it was just the shadow of death putting us on our best behavior. (My father had recently had a double bypass, and as soon as he recovered, my mother had a double mastectomy.) It is amazing how agreeable you can be when you fear that every word you say could be the last word someone hears.

On the plane home to Denver, I felt relieved and relaxed. We watched a silly movie, and I drank a miniature carafe of wine. By the time we left the Denver airport it was late, long past Grace's bedtime. She slept with her head in my lap, her open mouth imprinting a wet rose on the fabric of my skirt during the long ride home. Andrew and I sang along to Linda Ronstadt on the tape deck. It was a hot, dry night, and as we turned the corner to our street, Andrew said, "Let's go for a swim after we put Grace to bed." I nodded and smiled, thinking that after a week of sleeping in the same room with Grace at my parents' cottage, he had more in mind than just a swim.

When we pulled into the driveway, I noticed that the mail had overflowed its box and was piled haphazardly on the doorstep. Inside the house, while Andrew carried Grace upstairs to bed, I walked from room to room, opening the windows and taking an unconscious inventory. I noticed the Boston fern looked peaked, and when I stuck my finger in the soil, it was as dry as the Kalahari. I was spritzing the plants when Andrew reappeared stark naked carrying two towels.

"I thought Elka would be more reliable," I said, heading for the kitchen to refill the atomizer. "I'm surprised."

"Come on," he said. "You can do that later."

Outside, I slipped off my sweaty clothes. Andrew was already swimming minilaps. I waded into the cool water. It was perfectly quiet and dark, except for the soft splashing and the white-goose lamp glowing in Grace's upstairs window. Andrew surfaced beside me.

"Looks like they had a little party," he said, gesturing to a couple of overturned lawn chairs.

"Maybe it was the wind." I still wanted to believe that our neighbors were trustworthy.

"A real blow-out affair."

I groaned and he tried to duck me. We made practiced love in the shallow end of the pool and then went to bed and slept peacefully. In retrospect I would like to say we tossed and turned, that we were both visited by morbid nightmares, but, in truth, we slept peacefully. The next morning, while we were eating breakfast, the telephone rang. "You get it," I told Andrew. I was busy buttering toast and arguing with Grace about how much sugar belonged on her cereal. Suddenly Andrew hung up, clamped my arm, and propelled me into the hallway.

"What the hell . . . ?" I started to shake loose, then noticed his expression. An internal siren started wailing in the back of my brain, speeding forward.

"That was Nigel," he said. "He called to tell us Max drowned last Sunday. The day we left." He let go of my arm.

"No." I pressed my hands against my ears and shut my eyes as if it were some scary part of a movie that would be over with in a second, only it was worse with my eyes closed, projecting my own images. I opened them again.

He nodded, not saying anything, keeping his eyes locked on mine, not blinking, until the precise instant he saw it hit me, the rest of it.

"Oh Jesus," I said. "Not here." I looked out through the sunny kitchen, through the sliding glass doors, at the bright shimmer of turquoise. "How?"

"I don't know. Nigel didn't say and I didn't want to ask."

"Last night," I shuddered. "How could we not have *felt* something, something in the water, how could we . . ." I started to howl—a low, throaty growl that taxied slowly from my belly to my throat, then took off. He tried to wrap his arms around me, but I slapped them away. My fingernail scraped the inside of his wrist.

Grace bolted out of her chair and raced into the hallway clutching a piece of greasy toast. "What's wrong with Mommy?" Her eyes widened. She seemed to freeze in place.

"She hurt herself," Andrew said, staring aggrieved at the razor-thin thread of blood on his wrist. "She bumped her head." He bent over and picked Grace up. "You've got a jam mustache, Amazing Grace. Let's go shave it off."

"How'd she bump her head?" Grace asked suspiciously, looking back at me over his shoulder as he carted her off.

I opened the sliding glass doors and walked outside. The sun glinting off the water hurt my eyes. It looked exactly the same. A few leaves floating on the surface, a kick-board bobbing in the deep end. I don't know what I expected to see: blood, skid marks, broken glass? I looked over at Elka's house.

This is how it happened. (I heard the story first from another neighbor and later, in more detail, from Elka herself.) It was Sunday afternoon. We had just taken off. Elka and Max were in the kitchen, and Nigel was floating in his chaise lounge

in our pool. Elka, who hated to cook, was making some elaborate dessert for a dinner party that evening—the kind that re-
quires four hands to whip the egg whites, melt the chocolate,
sift the sugar, and de-stem the strawberries simultaneously.
Max was kneeling on a chair at the table, stabbing some Saltines
with peanut butter. I can picture his sticky fist pushing his
white-blond hair out of his eyes, his peanut-butter-coated
bangs spiked out like a punk rocker's. The phone rang and
Elka answered it, cradling the receiver between her shoulder
and neck as she continued to whip and melt and sift. It was
long distance, Nigel's widowed mother in London. As she
looked at the chocolate bubbling in the double boiler and as-
sured Mother Bentley that they were all fine, she told Max,
sotto voce, to run next door and tell Daddy to hurry to the
phone. After five or so minutes, when neither Nigel nor Max
had appeared, she apologized to her mother-in-law and said
Nigel would have to call her back. Irritated, she hung up,
turned the burners off, and cut across the backyard to our
house. The gate was open, and she could see Nigel in his floating lounge chair. She hollered, but he didn't answer. More irritated, she stormed over to the pool. As she neared the water's
edge, she could see that Nigel was wearing his Walkman, sound
asleep, his book open in his lap, snoring. Max was nowhere in
sight. Her heart started pounding in her ears like a movie
sound track, and she hollered Max's name as she stooped to
pick up the long-handled butterfly net we used to skim leaves
and bugs from the water's surface and extended the pole to
prod Nigel in the ribs. At that instant, out of the corner of her
eye, she spotted Max's red-and-blue-striped T-shirt floating
near the bottom of the pool, not far from Nigel's chaise lounge,
in the deep end. She dropped the pole and dove for him. The
pole clattering onto the cement jolted Nigel awake.

I began spending time with Elka. I didn't know what to say.
Under normal circumstances, I am not a demonstrative person, and had Elka been dry-eyed and glacial in her grief, as I

imagine I might have been in her place, most likely I would have mumbled my inadequate formal apologies and then avoided her out of guilt and embarrassment. But Elka's grief was a force of nature—a flood, a quake, an avalanche of emotion—that swept us both up. There was nothing personal or private about it. That first terrible evening when I knocked tentatively on her door, trembling with irrational guilt, expecting her to call me abusive names and slap us with a lawsuit, she flung open the door and embraced me. I could see that she had been sitting there in the dark, surrounded by little piles of Max's clean clothes. A plastic laundry basket was in the middle of the living room floor next to a box of Kleenex. We drank a whole bottle of Amaretto together—the only liquor in the house—tears streaming, not bothering to light a lamp as the dusk deepened into darkness inside the house. Nigel was not at home and somehow I did not think to ask where he was. I found it impossible to talk. I had never been particularly fluent in the language of the emotions. To me, words expressed thoughts, not feelings. Embarrassed by my silence, I got up and roamed into the kitchen. A pan of crusted chocolate was sitting on the stove, a bowl of spoiled egg-whites on the counter, wilted strawberries in the sink. The fact that Elka, normally such a compulsively neat hausfrau, had let her kitchen deteriorate to this state shook something loose inside me. I began washing the dishes, and as I stood at Elka's sink and plunged my hands into the hot soapy water, I experienced a terrifying disorientation, as if I *were* Elka, trapped in my grief, and not just the neighbor come to offer my condolences. I let Elka talk. She sat at the kitchen table, pouring us snifters of Amaretto, and rambled from one topic to the next, a frantic chatter not at all like her usual slow and soothing speech. She was passed out on the couch when I left around midnight, and I threw up in the bushes outside our back door before staggering inside.

After that, hardly an evening went by that I did not stray over there. Sitting at my desk reading about male-female roles in New Guinea or puberty rites among the Zuñi Indians, my thoughts would wander to Elka sitting there alone, and I would stare out my window at the pool, floodlit with an eerie greenish light. If I stared long enough, I would see a small shadow take shape under the surface of the water, like the outline of a murder victim drawn in chalk. I tried moving my desk to face the wall, but I just found myself putting away my books and joining Elka earlier every evening. I told myself this was my fieldwork in the land of grief, more foreign to me even than Pago Pago. I refused to let Grace come with me. Whenever Elka saw us together, I felt embarrassed, as if a starving person had caught me eating a steak. Since Andrew worried and complained about my spending so much time with Elka, I began to lie—to say I was going to the store or to the library or for a walk. There was only so much he could say without sounding hard-hearted. What soft-hearted person can begrudge a grieving mother? It occurred to me that there was a hole in the language. Why was there no word like *widow* to designate the mother of a dead child?

Elka would open a bottle of wine. Nigel was always out somewhere, probably at his lab, even after midnight. They were no comfort to each other. Sometimes she would take my hand and hold it, just hold it, and I would pat her hand, stiffly at first, then less so, as the wine unstarched me. There was nothing sexual about it. We were mourners. We could have been orphaned children or ninety-year-old widows. There was something ancient and collective at work. At the end of the month, Nigel rented a furnished apartment clear across the city, packed a suitcase, a few cartons of books and tools, and was gone. Statistics show that few marriages, even healthy ones, survive the death of a child. Elka didn't seem to miss him, rarely mentioned him. In the evolution of her life, he was like some secondary characteristic—a fin or gill—that, having ceased to serve a function, disappeared.

Andrew and I argued over the swimming pool. What I wanted to do, what I dreamed one night, was that we shoveled dirt into it like an open grave, until it was filled, and then we planted grass. However, we were renting the house and I knew the landlord would object. So I figured I would do the next best thing. While Andrew was on a wood-buying trip, I called the pool maintenance company and had them drain and cover the pool. This was mid-August, still hot enough to swim for several more weeks. Andrew arrived home in the late afternoon, tired and sweaty. He kissed me hello and then went upstairs to unpack. I didn't say anything even when he came down a few minutes later in his bathing trunks. Grace was across the street at a friend's birthday party. She had been pouting ever since the pool man came. My nerves were bad, and I had actually slapped her across the face that morning, then cried until she patted my hair to comfort me. Andrew slid the glass doors open and stepped outside. My stomach muscles clenched.

"Okay," he said, "Okay," when he walked back inside a split second later. "Okay." His voice was calm, soothing, as if he were gentling a spooked horse.

"You don't mind?" In the back of my brain, I heard my breathing kick on again.

"Did you think I would?"

"I don't know. I thought you might," I said. "You want a cold beer?"

"I want a cold swim!" He pounded the oak table with his fist so hard that the bowl of fruit bounced and two tangerines rolled onto the floor. "That's what I *want*, as if you cared."

"If you had any feelings, you wouldn't set foot in that pool," I shouted back. "The sight of it would make you sick."

"You're sick," he jabbed a finger at my chest. "You're obsessed." He dropped his hands to his sides suddenly, and the anger seemed to drain out through his fingertips. "Maybe you ought to see someone, a psychologist," he said more calmly. "This guilt—it's ridiculous. We had nothing to do with it. Nothing."

"I'm perfectly sane. I just don't like looking at that pool."

I knelt down and retrieved the bruised tangerines. "We survived without a pool for ten years. Most of the free world lives without swimming pools in their backyard."

"That's not the point."

I shrugged.

"I think we should move," he said. "Find another house."

"No!" I rummaged in the refrigerator for two beers and attempted a more calm and pragmatic tone. "We're settled. Grace has friends here."

"Yeah, and what about your friend?" His thumb stabbed the air in the direction of Elka's house. "Whatever's going on between the two of you isn't healthy."

"There's nothing 'going on.' Do I have to remind you that you're the one who had something 'going on'?"

"That's old news. Don't try to shift the blame." He twisted the cap off his beer and took a swallow. "I can see what's happening even if you can't."

The argument never really ended. It twisted and turned and splintered and mutated, destructive and indestructible. Almost every evening, Andrew would pack his gym bag and drive to the university, where he would swim laps for an hour. He had always been a half-hearted jogger, an on-again-off-again tennis player—never a swimmer. I knew he did it as a silent reproach. I didn't care. When Elka asked me whether Andrew minded my spending so much time with her, I said, "Of course not." And she believed me because he was always so friendly and helpful—mowing her lawn, fixing the leaky faucet. Even as late as November, when we were barely speaking, he got out the ladder and put up all her storm windows.

One evening, an unusually stifling August night, Andrew mixed up a pitcher of margaritas and we sat on the side patio, drinking and sweating. We avoided the backyard. The sight of the boarded-up pool only reminded us of our differences. Grace was already in bed. We were talking lightly about this and that, nothing much, and he reached over and pulled the

string on my bathing suit top. It slid down to my waist, and he
fished an ice cube out of his drink and began sliding it over my
breasts. The side porch was screened off by a tall hedge, and
when we first moved in, we had made love there once or
twice—Andrew liked the sensation of freedom—but I had
checked one day recently and discovered it was possible for
Elka to see us from her bedroom window. He slid his hand
under the waistband of my shorts and his icy fingertips sent a
shiver through me. I could see the light on in Elka's bedroom
and hear her radio playing softly.

"Not here," I said. "Inside."

"It's too hot in there." He knelt down on the flagstone and
put his face between my legs. I moaned, then thought of Elka
over there all alone, listening to us, and pushed him away.

"What's the matter?" he said.

"Elka. I don't want her to see us."

"Why? You think she'd be jealous?" He flung my bathing suit
top at me.

"No. I think she'd feel sad."

"Christ, I'm tired of this." He stood up and slid open the
glass door into our bedroom. "Max may have drowned, but
you're in way over your head." He slammed the door behind
him, stormed into the bathroom, and turned on the shower. It
sounded like heavy rain. I looked at the sky expecting to hear
thunder and see lightning.

In September, I began teaching, Grace started second grade,
and Andrew's father, Art the Fart, suffered a mild stroke. A retired Air Force colonel, he had rarely spoken a civil word
to Andrew, his only son, since he filed for C.O. status in 1968,
but Andrew promptly flew out to Monterey when his mother
called with the news. I suspected that he welcomed the excuse
to get away for a while, since for no rational reason things
were deteriorating so rapidly between us. It was almost as if
we were the ones who had lost our child, and occasionally

when I passed by Grace's room, I would experience this chill of desolation, as if she were long dead. It was as if because the tragedy had taken place in our backyard, it was somehow meant for us; we were part owners.

It was not a good time for Andrew to be gone. I sometimes wonder if everything might simply, gradually have returned to normal if Andrew had not jumped at the first chance to escape. This may sound naive, but I believe in the domino theory— the chain reaction. At any point along the way, the chain can be broken, resistance can halt momentum. But Andrew had never been a fighter. Look how effortlessly he had relinquished his lover, the woman in San Francisco. At the time I interpreted it as a sign of his caring (for me), but later I realized it was a sign of his not caring (for her)—at least not enough to resist—and Elka was in no shape to resist anything. So that left me. Grief and love feel a lot alike, different stages of the same emotion. It's difficult to tell them apart in the dark.

With Andrew in California, someone needed to be there for Grace on the afternoons I taught my Intro class and the two evenings a week I conducted the honors seminar. Elka volunteered. After school, Grace went next door and played with Elka's collection of old German dolls—real glass eyes and human hair—while Elka worked at her floor loom. When I returned home, Elka would have a savory stew simmering on the stove, a crisp salad in the refrigerator.

"I thought you hated to cook," I said the first evening. "You don't have to do all this."

"I need to keep busy," she said. "It's good for me."

The evenings I had my seminar Elka would stay after dinner. She would watch television or play Chinese checkers with Grace until her bedtime. I had feared that Grace's presence would be a constant, wounding reminder of Max's absence, but Elka seemed to seek her out, and sometimes I would hear them laughing together about something silly. One afternoon I came home and found Elka sitting on the couch with Grace sound asleep in her lap. Elka was stroking Grace's hair, the same white-blond as Max's, weeping silently. Grace woke up as soon as I entered the room and burst into frightened tears when she saw Elka crying. Andrew and I had sat Grace down and explained to her about Max's being dead. She had listened somberly and then said, "Like Weenie?" Weenie was our dachshund, the one who had been run over, so we figured that she understood.

None of us seemed capable of sleeping alone in our solitary beds, of getting through the night. Elka postponed returning to her empty house later and later each night, until it seemed only logical that she stay. The third bedroom was my study and the couch was too short for Elka's long legs, so she slept in my bed. We balanced precariously like bookends on either edge of the bed, chaste as schoolgirls, more chaste, waiting for Grace. Grace's nightmares started while Andrew was in California. Almost every night she would wake up choking and crying, not screaming, and stumble into my bedroom. "I want Daddy," she'd whimper, then still half-asleep, she would curl up between Elka and me in bed, her body like a tight little fist, and the three of us would huddle like aborigines around a fire in the darkness, only we *were* the fire.

I had not spoken to Andrew since he called to say he had arrived safely in Monterey, his father seemed strong and alert, and his parents were driving him crazy. A cautious, civil conversation. After that, a postcard arrived every other day or so. He had been gone ten days. The last postcard said he was visiting friends of ours in Berkeley. It was postmarked San Francisco, which could have signified anything—dinner in Chinatown, an old movie at the Surf Theater, linguine and clams at Little Joe's in North Beach. We had been married ten years and lived together for two before that. You would think that after twelve years you would just *know* one way or the other, but I had no idea if he were seeing her again or not—the woman with the Italian virginal. Her name was Maggie.

As it turned out, or at least as he told me and I believe him, he had not even called her, although he had been to the city for dinner two or three times and had thought about it each time. He had told the whole story about Max and Elka and me to Peter, his former partner, over Irish coffees at the Buena Vista one evening. Peter had listened and then said, "So what's the problem? I don't get it. She feels sorry for this Elka, she spends a lot of time with her. It's a temporary situation. Let it ride."

"There's more to it," Andrew said, immediately defensive.

"What?" Peter asked. "I'm listening."

"I don't know. I don't know," Andrew laughed. "There must be something."

"And suddenly I just felt ridiculous," Andrew said when he called me from the pay phone at the Buena Vista. "I can't even remember why I've been so angry. I was trying to explain it to Peter and suddenly it just seemed like no big deal. I guess I just overreacted. I'm sorry."

"It's just been a bad time," I said. "For all of us."

"How's Elka?"

"Better," I said.

"Good. Are you still spending as much time with her?" His voice had a slight edge, although he was trying to keep it light.

"Not so much. I'm busy with classes," I mumbled.

"What?" he shouted.

I could hear loud music and talking and laughter and the clatter of dishes in the background. Elka was asleep on the couch in front of the television, where I'd found her when I came home from my seminar, and Grace was upstairs in bed. I didn't want to shout.

I cupped my hand around the mouthpiece and whispered into it. "I said not so much. We hardly see each other. Where are you?"

"The Buena Vista. I guess Peter was right. He said, in effect, I was being a jerk."

"You're not a jerk," I said. "And even if you are, I miss you."

"I miss you, too. In fact, I'm thinking . . ."

There was a loud crash, as if someone had dropped a tray full of silverware at Andrew's feet. "I can't hear you," I said.

"Never mind," he shouted. "This is ridiculous. Call you later." He hung up.

The phone call cheered me. Everything seemed lighter suddenly, as if a simple solution for some weighty problem had just occurred to me, and I hummed an old Linda Ronstadt song as I climbed the stairs and ran the water for my bath. I carried the radio into the bathroom and submerged myself in the steamy water, thinking over responses I wished I had given to student questions earlier in the evening. Whenever the bath water cooled off, I'd rotate the *Hot* faucet with my toes and let it blast until I was pleasantly scalded again. I thought about all the times Andrew had marveled and complained about my capacity to withstand heat. And I remembered a documentary about nuclear radiation in which this activist nun said that if you heated it up gradually, frogs would remain in a pot of water until they boiled themselves to death. This was supposed to be a metaphor for humanity and the arms race. When I finished draining the bath and drying myself off, I tiptoed into my bedroom for a clean nightgown. Elka and Grace were already sound asleep in bed, nestled together in the pitch dark like two small, furry animals trying to burrow into the same hole.

Hours later, Elka was shaking me. It was still dark. I was dreaming that we were swimming in the ocean in Florida, near my parents' house. Max and my father were floating in a large black inner tube garlanded with flowers.

"I heard something," Elka whispered. "Someone's downstairs."

I sat up quickly, my heart hammering, and covered Grace completely with the blanket, as if to make her invisible to danger. I heard the footsteps on the stairs. Elka and I sat there frozen. I couldn't decide if it would be better or worse to turn on the light. Where's Andrew? I thought, panicked and paralyzed, and then there he was, standing in the doorway, whispering my name: "Jane, Jane? It's Andrew. Are you awake?"

"Thank God!" I burst out and snapped on the bedside lamp. "You scared us half to death." I pressed the palm of my hand against my heart. "Be still." I was laughing with relief. He was standing there staring, glaring really, as Elka nervously buttoned the top button of her pajamas and Grace suddenly woke up and shouted, "Daddy!" She leapt out of bed and ran after him as he stormed down the stairs. I could hear their voices but not their words down below in the kitchen. Elka and I looked at each other, not quite meeting each other's eyes. For the first time I felt awkward with her. I was aware of the weight of my breasts through the thin nightgown material, and I could smell her spicy perfume on the sheets. She reached over and covered my hand with hers, a gesture of comfort, and for the first time I felt the charge between us, as if my blood were slowly heating up, and it surprised me and alarmed me. I felt Elka's trembling pass through me, and I wondered where this came from. It was as if our passion were a figment of Andrew's jealousy.

Andrew flew back to California the next day. He stayed away. He would call to talk to Grace but refuse to speak to me. He gave Grace a phone number where she could reach him and told her it was a secret. While she was at school, I searched her room until I found it taped inside the lid of her jewelry box. I left the lid open, and, sitting on my bed, I could hear the tinkly silver music through the wall as I dialed the number. A woman answered. "Hello," I said. "Andrew Lefler gave me your name as a reference. I'm thinking of buying a harpsichord."

"Oh yes," she said. "What would you like to know?"

I hung up.

He called me that evening from a pay phone. It must have

been on the street. I could hear traffic noises. "What do you want?" he kept saying. "Do you really want me to come back?"

"Yes," I said. "Yes, yes, yes. How many times do I have to say it."

"All right. Two conditions. One, you find yourself a therapist. Two, you find us another house."

"Okay. How soon can you be here?" I said. "I want you to come right away."

"What's the rush? You sound scared."

"I *am* scared," I shouted, then lowered my voice. "Tomorrow? Can you come tomorrow?"

"I told you. Two conditions. I'm not coming back until—"

"You're not serious," I interrupted.

"I *am* serious. I want to know *you're* serious. Are you?"

I didn't answer right away. I stood up and paced the room. Out the window I could see the swimming pool cover sagging under a blanket of brown leaves.

"I'll call the landlord tomorrow," I said.

But I didn't. I couldn't imagine Elka living next door to strangers or the house standing empty. Nigel called her periodically. He even stopped by the house with plane tickets one evening and begged her to go away on vacation with him to Hawaii, but she refused and asked him not to come back. She spent most of her time at our house. I don't know what the neighbors thought. I don't know what we thought. We tried not to think about it, to label it. Once in the heat of a long-distance argument, Andrew called me a "dyke," and I was literally winded by the insult.

"It's not like that," I shouted and hung up, furious, then ran to the bathroom and threw up. I was too sick to come to the phone when he called back five minutes later. Elka answered it and said he'd said to tell me he was sorry. I was stretched out on the tile floor. She knelt down and sponged my face and neck with a cool washcloth. Her long hair tickled my arm.

I reached up and tucked a strand back behind her ear. In the winter her hair was the color of sand and the exposed ear as delicately pink as a shell. I imagined lying next to her, pressing my ear to hers, lulled by the distant hush of ocean. She locked the door and lay down next to me on the cold tiles.

At Thanksgiving Andrew came back for five days to visit with Grace and collect his things. Elka flew to St. Paul to have Thanksgiving with her parents and brother's family. While she was away, Andrew put up her storm windows and sawed some dead limbs off the massive tree in her front yard. He no longer seemed angry, just sad—bewildered but resigned. I had papers to grade and was not in a festive mood, so the three of us had Thanksgiving dinner in a restaurant and then escorted Grace to a matinee of *Snow White* where she sat between us. Andrew and I slept in our bed and even made love twice, the first night and the last, hello and good-bye. He was going to London with Maggie—she had some grant and he was going to study harpsichord making at the London College of Furniture, something he had always wanted to do. He agreed to let Grace stay with me, temporarily at least. I promised to send her to a child psychologist once a week and to have the psychologist send him monthly reports. Part of me bristled at being put on probation like this, but another part of me was relieved to have some professional monitoring the situation, which, as far as I was concerned, was already way beyond my control. I thought of it as a kind of emotional avalanche, something apart from me, with a momentum all its own. A fluke. Something that could not happen again in a million years. Something that is neither happy nor sad. Something that defies definition.

The week after Andrew left, Elka moved in. We carried the dining room set down to the basement and moved her loom into the empty space. In my study, directly above the dining room, I can hear the shuttle slamming back and forth, back and forth. Elka works at a furious pace, as if she is trying to make up for lost time. Lately, she has begun reading through my anthropology books, which are filled with descriptions of women weaving—mats, baskets, textiles. Inspired by Elka, I am gathering notes for a scholarly paper on the role of weaving in tribal cultures. And inspired by me, she is working on a series of "mosquito bags" modeled after the elaborate, highly prized sleeping bags the Tchambuli women in New Guinea used to weave. Two of these woven bags equaled the price of one canoe.

And even Grace has developed a sudden, passionate interest in weaving. Elka has given her a small hand loom. Often, when I gravitate downstairs for a snack or study break, I find Grace sitting cross-legged on the floor next to Elka, working away on some narrow, brightly colored belt or scarf. Their hands seem to dance in the slanting afternoon light as they work side by side in companionable silence. It is a peaceful scene— primitive, archetypal, female—and for one perfect instant I imagine the men are off in their canoes, catching fish with their bare hands. And any moment now they will appear, Andrew and Nigel holding aloft the canoe, and Max bringing up the rear, clutching the fish to his chest, the day's bountiful catch shining silver in the bright sun.

Movie Music

"And you know what else is weird?" It is two A.M. and I am propped up on one elbow in bed, chatting into the dark, still high from all the drinking and joking. I just quit nursing Nicole and tonight was the first time I've been smashed in over a year.

My husband, Charlie, turns his back on me. "No," he says, like I am looking for an answer instead of a question.

I don't know why he does that. It always puts me in a bad mood. I feel all the fizz go out of me, like a glass of flat Coke. I just lie there in the dark wishing I were someone else somewhere else with someone else.

Earlier in the evening we had laughed ourselves sick playing the Baby Boomer edition of Trivial Pursuit with Charlie's brother, Clem, and my best friend, Janelle. After they went home (separately), we'd watched the tail end of Johnny Carson in bed and made love. It was the first time I had agreed to keep the light on since Nicole was born five months ago. We had gone to Lamaze class and I had quit smoking and drinking and started swimming laps at the Y every morning, but when the time came, I had to have an emergency cesarean, just as if I'd sat around for nine months watching TV and drinking Jim Beam. At the time, after twenty-six hours of labor, I wouldn't have cared if they'd gutted me like a fish, but I cried a couple of days later when they changed the bandage and I got a good look at the scar. I was expecting a bikini incision like my sister Deborah has. The nurse explained to me how in emergency cases like mine, where the monitor shows fetal distress, the doctor doesn't have time for cosmetics. The scar looked like a maroon zipper.

Suddenly, thinking about the scar and all I went through, I feel a powerful jolt of anger. I snap on the lamp next to the bed. "I'm talking to you," I say.

He flings his arm over his eyes. "Okay, so what's so goddamn weird?"

I am tempted to ignore him.

"I'm all ears." He yawns, overexaggerating, like a silent-screen star. "You were saying . . . ?"

I reach over to the night table and screw the cap on my K-Y jelly, which is leaking onto the embroidered dresser scarf my sister brought us back from Communist China.

"I'm in love with Clem and we're going to live together," I say. "Nicole, Clem, and me. In California," I add, even though this, none of this, has ever even crossed my mind before and has nothing to do with what I had originally intended to say, which was that Janelle had not missed one single question all evening and I suspected that since Richard had left her and gone back to his wife again she was sitting at home alone at night, listening to the radio and memorizing the answers to the Trivial Pursuit questions. The minute I hear this thing I've said, though, about Clem and me, I know it is going to come true, one way or another. I can feel it in my scar.

Charlie rolls over facing me. He laughs, like it is a big joke. "Jesus, woman, what's got into you?" He pretends like he's unzipping my scar. "Zip, zip."

"Don't toy with me!" I shout, furious. I fling his arm off me. I hear his knuckles thwack against the mahogany headboard. He tucks his bruised hand under his armpit.

"I'm sorry," I whisper. "I didn't mean to."

"I know it." He reaches over his arm and pulls me to him. "You're drunk, baby." He strokes my hair and massages my temples. "You're going to have one hell of a hangover."

I start to cry. A tear dribbles into my mouth. It tastes like straight Jim Beam.

"Shhh," he says. "Go to sleep."

The baby in the next room starts to wail. I go to comfort her, but as I am holding her soft warm body with its sweet baby smell, it's not clear to me who is comforting who.

Nothing has changed, but suddenly I am extremely anxious, I am walking on eggshells. It's as if my normal life has turned into one of those scary movies, like *Psycho* or *Wait until Dark*. As I change Nicole's diaper or fix dinner, I can hear the movie music running through my head like a sound track—that kind of nerve-jarring music they use to keep you on the edge of your seat. I jump every time the phone rings or a car door slams outside. I spend a lot of time peeking out at the street, hidden behind my drapes.

One Saturday afternoon I hear a car door slam and peek out through the lace bedroom curtains to see Clem coming up the walk. He is wearing jeans and a sweater I'd knit for Charlie that turned out too small for him, and his normally bushy hair is slicked back, wet. Without his wild hair, he looks kind of pathetic, like a dog after a bath. As he walks up the front steps and rings the doorbell, I hold my hand over Nicole's mouth and rock her so she won't cry. He waits a minute, puzzled because he sees my old Valiant in the driveway, then leaves a paper bag on the front porch. As his Pinto turns the corner, I get the bag from the porch. I take out Charlie's electric drill, which Clem borrowed a while back, and a bag of dried pineapple—my favorite—from the health food store where he works a few hours a week while he is studying to be a chiropractor. When he gets his degree, he plans to open his own office on the beach in Santa Barbara, buy a VW convertible, and grow a beard.

I head for the kitchen, but for no reason at all I decide to hide the pineapple at the bottom of the laundry basket. Then I dress Nicole warmly and take her for a walk to the drugstore in her stroller, hoping she will fall asleep and nap for a couple of hours so that I can soak in a hot tub and maybe relax with a new magazine or two before it's time to start dinner.

On the way back, we stroll past the high school. Some boys are out on the field, waiting for football practice. One boy with blond hair runs up and down the bleachers, surefooted as a mountain goat. He reminds me of Charlie, how he was when I started going out with him senior year in high school. I had hung around the bleachers every afternoon watching him practice. Whenever he would look over at me, I would look away, and whenever he saw me looking at him, he would pretend to be looking beyond me, at some invisible object in the distance. Finally he had told a friend of his who told his girlfriend who told one of my girlfriends who told me that he wouldn't mind going out with me. Whereupon I told my girlfriend who told her girlfriend who told her boyfriend who told Charlie that I wouldn't mind going out with him.

We went to a drive-in movie and then drove out and sat by the Cedar River and confessed that we loved each other. We didn't have much to talk about in the beginning, so I remember he used to read me postcards from his older brother, Clem, who had hitchhiked to San Francisco and was crashing in a big old house near the Golden Gate Park, making roach clips out of brass wire and beads. I remember I had no idea what a roach clip was. Charlie said it must be some sort of trap for cockroaches and speculated that the brightly colored beads lured the roaches into the metal traps.

Once, when Charlie's parents were away, we went up to his room and I saw some pictures of Clem. He looked skinny and pale, and I remember telling Charlie that I thought he was much better looking than his brother. I guess that was just the encouragement he needed because he suddenly tackled me right there in his room. He pulled me down on the lower bunk bed and that was the first time we actually did it, although we had been doing everything else but for months.

About the time Charlie and I started sleeping together, Clem went on down to Mexico, and the postcards took weeks, sometimes months, to arrive. I liked the looks of Mexico on the postcards and hinted around that it looked like a good place to go for a honeymoon. Charlie's father kept threatening to go down to Mexico and drag Clem back, but we knew it was just talk. Mr. Knupfer had never been outside of Iowa in his life and didn't even like Chinese food.

After Mexico, Clem got himself a job on a ship going to Europe and Charlie got one of those thin aerograms with a red and blue border. I remember holding it and sniffing it and examining the ingenious way the paper turned right into an envelope. I had taken French in high school and I was proud of myself for knowing what *Par Avion* meant.

From Europe, Clem went on to India, and by the time he finally arrived home with hepatitis, Charlie and I were already married and living in a two-bedroom apartment in Des Moines. Charlie and I were working days at the same department store—he worked in Furniture and I worked in Toys. Clem moved in with us for a few weeks, while he was gaining his strength back. When he was bored, he used to walk downtown to the department store and visit us. He would sit in the Barca-lounger up on the fourth floor with Charlie and watch the row of TV's for sale. Then he would take the escalator down to Toys and walk around reading the game boxes or trying out the remote-control cars while I waited on customers. He was good with kids and played right along with them so that their mothers had to practically drag them kicking and screaming out of the store, away from Clem.

Nights, Charlie went to business school and Clem and I would sit at home playing Clue or Risk or some other game I had purchased with my employee discount. My favorite was Risk. We would sit at opposite ends of the table, with the world spread out between us, and as his conquering armies invaded one country after another, Clem would tell me amusing stories about his adventures in Baja or Yugoslavia or Nepal.

One weekend when Charlie went duck hunting in Michigan with two friends from the business school, Clem and I spent two nights alone in the apartment together. The first night we drove to Iowa City, where the university is, to see this French movie that Clem wanted to see. I was nervous because I had never seen a movie with subtitles before, but as soon as the movie started, I forgot it wasn't in English. It was the strangest thing. Afterward I told Clem I didn't believe I had been reading subtitles; I believed that for two hours God had let me understand French. We were drinking wine at a coffee house near campus. I noticed how Clem fit in there with his tied-back long hair, his Indian shirt and water buffalo sandals. Charlie and I had always thought of him as an exotic misfit, but suddenly I felt like the misfit in my dressy dress, nylons, and patent leather pumps.

The second night Clem cooked me some chicken curry and played me some songs he'd written on his guitar. Then he brought out a couple of joints from the pocket of his embroidered workshirt. Charlie didn't like him to smoke in the apartment, but I knew he smoked in his room after we'd gone to bed. I could smell it when I got up to go to the bathroom in the middle of the night. I had smoked a couple of times with friends, but this stuff was stronger. He said it was from Thailand. I felt like everything was suddenly more than it usually was: brighter, louder, bigger, funnier, scarier, closer. I felt like I'd suddenly lost the knack of being myself—I couldn't remember where to put my hands, what to say, how to stop smiling. Clem suggested we go for a walk. I put on my coat and we must have walked five miles while Clem pointed out the constellations and told me stories about when he and Charlie were growing up. I felt like I understood more about Charlie during that walk than I'd understood in the year and a half I'd been his wife, but part of it must just have been the marijuana, because when Charlie came back from Michigan the next day, all those big insights I'd had seemed all shriveled up, like pricked balloons.

When we got back inside the house from our walk, Clem took my hand at the bottom of the stairs and looked right into my eyes, right into me. No one had ever looked at me like that, not even Charlie. He kissed me on the forehead where he'd told me the Third Eye was, and then he kind of spun me around and pushed me up the stairs. He stayed downstairs while I used the bathroom and got into Charlie's and my bed. I heard him playing music downstairs till all hours. When I got up in the morning, he was asleep on the couch and the turntable was spinning silently.

Once he was all recovered, Clem borrowed some money from us, bought himself a Harley Davidson, and went back to California. We didn't see much of him after that for five or six years. He and Charlie kept in touch with an occasional postcard or phone call on holidays. We moved back home to Cedar Rapids. Clem went to one of those state universities out there and got a degree in film, then moved to Hollywood and wrote us that he was working as a gaffer, a lighting man, in television. He was married once for a few months, but they were already divorced by the time Charlie and I flew out there for a week's vacation one summer.

Clem worked till all hours—he was working on "Laverne and Shirley"—so Charlie and I rented a car and drove up and down the coast. Charlie had just been promoted to manager of a new McDonald's in Des Moines, and we stopped at every McDonald's from LA to San Francisco until I threw a fit in Los Banos and threatened to stick my finger down my throat and throw up all over the next McDonald's we stopped in. After that Charlie seemed to lose interest in traveling, and we ended up going back to Clem's apartment two days early. I went to the studio lot and ate in the commissary with Clem, alert to the possibility of movie stars, while Charlie played golf with Clem's next-door neighbor.

On the plane ride home I told Charlie that I didn't think Clem seemed very happy. He didn't seem to have many friends and his place looked about as homey as a Motel 6 room. He didn't even own any pots and pans. "I think he's still in love with that wife of his," I said.

"I saw a picture of her. She wasn't so hot." Charlie signaled the stewardess for a second drink. "She was kind of puny looking."

"Maybe so," I said, "but he's not over her yet."

"He'll find himself someone else. A TV starlet." He tried to unscrew the cap of his doll-size scotch bottle. He had put on some weight in the past couple of years, and his hands seemed big and clumsy. "That's what I'd do in his shoes."

"Clem's not like you." I reached over and unscrewed the cap for him.

"That's right," Charlie winked. "I'm the good-looking one. You always said so."

"Really?" I said. "I'd forgotten." He laughed, but I really had.

Not long after that, Clem had some sort of nervous collapse and came home to Cedar Rapids for a rest. Charlie's father had died of a heart attack a few years back, so Clem moved into their old family house on Mulberry Avenue with his mother. She was glad to have him back and it took a load off of us, not having to worry that she would fall down the stairs and break her hip and lie there for days. He dug up the backyard and planted a big vegetable garden. When we asked him what he was planning to do for the future, he said he would let us know just as soon as he did. One day, six months or so later, he called us up, very excited, and said he'd decided to become a chiropractor. I remembered that he had injured his back lifting some heavy equipment in California and had gone to a chiropractor out there who cured his back pain. Clem seemed to think of this guy right up there with Albert Schweitzer. When he called, I was pregnant with Nicole and was having lower back pain myself. I imagined lying in a cool, quiet office with Clem's fingers magically massaging my spine, easing the strain.

Now the back pain is just a dim memory and Nicole is here, big as day, sitting in her stroller, chewing on her chubby fist. The high school boys have put on their helmets and are tossing the football back and forth. I wheel the stroller back and forth behind the barbed wire fence, keeping my eye on Number 11, the one who reminds me of Charlie. I shake out my hair, making sure none of it is caught under my jacket collar, and stand up straight, sucking in my stomach, which is still not as flat as it was before Nicole was born. The boy glances over but seems to look right through me. My smile collapses. I suppose to him I just look like someone's wife and mother out walking her baby.

When Charlie comes home that night, I have set my hair on hot rollers and brushed it upside down so that it floats around my face. I am wearing a low-cut sweater and my designer jeans. He whistles when he walks in the door, pinches my rear, and kisses the tops of my breasts. I sit on his lap in the kitchen while we wait for the noodles to cook. Nicole contentedly gums a rice cracker in her baby seat at the other end of the table. As I drain the noodles, I can feel the steam from the boiling water making my hair go limp, but I feel reassured that I still have a few good years left. I can feel Charlie's eyes glued to me as I sashay back and forth between the table and the stove in my backless high heels.

Ever since I said that crazy thing about Clem and me, I have been studying Charlie's behavior to see if it had any particular effect on him. You would think your wife tells you she's in love with your brother, that would get under your skin at least a little. Even if you thought she was kidding or drunk or something, it would still get to you—like when you answer a wrong number in the middle of the night, it just makes you uneasy. It's like the bad news you'd expected is still out there waiting for you. But as far as I can see, it just went in one ear and out the other. I am relieved, of course, but also a little miffed. It just seems typical somehow, although I can't think of anything like this that has ever happened before.

Unlike me, Charlie doesn't brood over things. With Charlie, what you see is what you get. So when he tells me he's invited Clem to dinner on Sunday, even though I can hear that creepy movie music in my ears and my heart flaps like birds' wings in my chest, I don't suspect him of any underhanded motive. He is holding Nicole on his lap, making funny faces at her. I walk over and kiss him lightly on the top of his head, where his thin hair is getting thinner. He smells faintly of french fries. His dream is to own his own franchise, and he has the site picked out, not far from the high school. Sometimes, lying in bed, he likes to fantasize about how when Nicole is in high school, he'll have his own McDonald's and Nicole will be able to bring all her friends by to eat for free after the football games.

The Wednesday before the Sunday that Clem is coming for dinner, Janelle stops by on her way from work. She teaches jazzercise at a fancy new health spa. She is all excited over this psychic one of the new women in her class told her about. The psychic predicted that the woman would become involved in the performing arts before the end of the year, and two weeks later she found a flier for Janelle's jazzercise class under the windshield wiper of her car while she was parked at the grocery store and decided to enroll. Janelle has the psychic's address and wants me to go along with her. I know what Janelle wants to know. She wants to know whether Richard is going to get bored with being faithful to his wife and come slinking back to Janelle. I could predict with absolute certainty that he will (since he always does) and save Janelle the five bucks, but I also know with absolute certainty that she won't listen to me.

The psychic lives in a ranch house in a new subdivision on the east side of town. She sits us down on her sofa in the living room and offers us some canned sodas and some corn Bugles. She has a six-month-old boy in a playpen in the corner of the dining room, and I unzip Nicole's jacket and put her in the playpen across from the boy. The two babies stare at each other in alarm.

The psychic's name is Marge. She looks too normal, I think, to be a convincing psychic. She is wearing khaki pants and a pink polo shirt and loafers. She doesn't use a crystal ball or cards or tea leaves—no props. She simply holds Janelle's hand loosely in her lap and looks at her intently. I can feel Janelle's faith wavering, although she *wants* to believe. Marge tells her some stuff that, at least in my opinion, is completely off the mark. She says that she can tell that Janelle is a very creative and spiritual person. (As far as I know, Janelle hasn't done anything creative since we made ashtrays together in third grade, and her idea of a higher being is Robert Redford.) She also tells her that the man she is involved with really loves her and will ask her to marry him by the end of the month. Marge says she sees a June wedding. Janelle is overjoyed, obviously having chosen to ignore the fact that Richard is already married to someone else and therefore could not possibly be marrying Janelle in June, two months from now, even if he wanted to, which everyone but Janelle can see he doesn't. Sometimes, like now, when I see Janelle acting so dense, I wonder why I have remained friends with her over the years.

"Now it's your turn," Janelle beams at me.

I hold out my hand dutifully. Marge cups her hands around mine and I feel a pleasant surge of energy. I like her even if she is a fake. It has been years since I've held a woman's hand, since my grandmother died, and I'm enjoying the cool, soft gentleness of her touch.

"You," she says, "don't belong here. I see you by the ocean. There are palm trees. It's hot, the sun is shining."

"Am I alone?" I whisper hoarsely.

"No," she says. "There's your little girl and a thin man with bushy hair and a beard."

"A beard?" Janelle shrugs, mystified, and raises her eyebrows at me. She insists on paying for both of us. In the car she says, "Amazing how she could be so on target with me and so off with you, isn't it?"

"Nobody's perfect," I say.

That night I can't sleep. In the middle of the night I walk downstairs to the kitchen in my nightgown and call my sister, Deborah, in Honolulu, not so much because we are close but because it is still only nine P.M. there. When her Irish live-in babysitter, what Deborah calls her "o'pair," answers, I remember how little we actually have in common, even if we are sisters. She is married to a real estate tycoon, her second marriage, and has gone back to school to get her master's degree in psychology. I almost never make long-distance calls, and when she first recognizes my voice, she sounds worried, braced for disaster. I have to assure her that Mom, Daddy, Granddad, Charlie, and Nicole are all fine before it occurs to her to ask me how I am.

"Something funny's going on here," I whisper. "I've got this bad feeling." As I explain to her, I keep looking over my shoulder and lowering my voice. She keeps saying "What?" and "Can't you speak louder?" I know that Charlie's sound asleep, but it feels like the walls have ears.

"Has anything, you know, actually *happened* between you and Clem?" she asks when I'm finished.

"No," I say. "Not a thing."

"It sounds to me like you *want* it to," she says. She is always saying things like that since she started studying psychology.

"I don't," I say. "I just feel like somehow it's *going* to. You know, like in a dream when someone's chasing you and you're running down this alley and that alley, and at the end of every alley you run smack into him."

"Are you saying that Clem is chasing you?"

"No," I sigh. I can tell this is useless. She doesn't understand. "It's this creepy feeling I have. Like it's in the cards, you know— fate or something. It's not just me. The psychic saw it, too."

"Hmmmn," Deborah says. "It reminds me of Oedipus. You know how he left town because of what the oracle said and then ended up sleeping with his mother anyway."

I can hear Nicole fussing in her bassinet upstairs. I grip the receiver tighter and will her to hush up. "How'd he end up sleeping with her if he'd gone away?" I ask.

"I forget," Deborah says. "It was just fate, like what you were saying. That's the point."

My heart is beginning to race. If Nicole starts to wail, Charlie will wake up. The two things in the world that get him most riled are being woken up and long-distance phone bills.

"I was thinking I might go away for a while, but I had this feeling it wouldn't make any difference," I say glumly.

"I think you're just worn out," she says. "I got that way after Cody was born. Your mind just—"

"I've got to go," I interrupt. "Nicole's crying."

"Take care," she says. "And don't worry."

Sunday is the first clear, warm day we've had in a week. Charlie wakes up in a good mood. When Nicole cries, he brings her into our bed and the three of us play hide and seek under the covers until Charlie sniffs Nicole's bottom and hands her to me. I get up, change her diaper, and dress her in a new pink sunsuit that my mother sent from Florida. After breakfast, Charlie mows the lawn, back and forth across the yard with Nicole strapped to his back like a papoose. I have to smile as I watch them out the laundry room window. Her sunbonnet has slipped to a crazy angle and her bright blue eyes take it all in, big as saucers. For a moment, as I dump the dirty clothes into the washer, I am so proud of my little family that I forget to feel afraid. I think maybe the psychic has me confused with someone else.

By five o'clock I have done the grocery shopping, cleaned the house, and marinated the chicken. When I take the clean clothes out of the dryer, I find the bag of dried pineapple, hardly any worse for the wear. I tear the bag open and put the pineapple in a blue bowl on the counter. Charlie is out back, drinking beer, tending the smoldering charcoal briquets. Nicole has finally, reluctantly, drifted off to sleep. I have an hour before Clem is due to arrive and I shout out to Charlie that I'll be in the shower.

As I undress, I am careful to avoid looking at my body in the full-length mirror on the door, and as I soap myself, I avoid touching the raised scar. When I go downstairs, dressed in fresh jeans and a new white blouse, Clem is already seated in a lawn chair by the grill. Seated next to him, through a cloud of smoke, I see a woman with curly blond hair, like mine. No one said anything to me about another guest. Mentally I count up the number of chicken parts, and even though there are enough for two pieces each, I am suddenly in a bad mood.

Clem stands up and gives me a bear hug. "This is Greta," he says, introducing the smiling blond woman. "When we met, I told her she reminded me of my sister-in-law. Don't you think so, Charlie?"

Charlie nods vaguely and begins slapping chicken pieces onto the grill. Greta and I smile at each other, probably each privately insulted. I know I am. We might have the same coloring, but she has at least fifteen pounds on me and is dressed like a guerrilla soldier.

"You know Clem for long?" I ask her, just as she's stuffing a deviled egg, which they brought, into her mouth.

"About three months," she says when she swallows. She smiles at Clem who is uncorking a bottle of wine.

"Three months!" I say, shocked. "Clem never said a word."

"He's a sly dog," Charlie winks and slaps a breast onto the grill.

"We met at a bookstore," Clem says. "We were buying the same book." He wraps his fingers lightly around hers as he pours wine into her glass. "You'll like this wine," he says to me. "Gewürtztraminer. Tastes like petunias."

I sip my wine without comment. Charlie sits down opposite us with his beer. He looks back and forth between Greta and me. "You two could be sisters all right." He waves his spatula in our direction. His eyes look a little out of focus, like he's having momentary difficulty remembering who is who.

I am mostly silent, except for an occasional snide comment, during dinner. However, no one notices, it seems, because

Greta is a nonstop talker. She talks about books and movies and foreign travel. She reminds me of that man in the Federal Express commercial, the speed-talker. Clem listens attentively and laughs a lot when she talks. Sometimes he disagrees with her opinions, which perks me up a little. Then, unfortunately for her, partway through dinner she makes the mistake of telling Charlie that her very first paying job was working at a McDonald's in Amsterdam. That's all Charlie needs to get him going on his favorite topic of conversation. Clem and I just exchange glances, smile, and roll our eyes.

I have drunk several glasses of wine by this point, and my mood has risen several notches. I am beginning to feel flattered that he chose a woman who looks like me, even such a poor copy, and the movie music in my head has gone away. I figure the psychic just got us confused. She saw blond hair and blue eyes and naturally assumed it was me. Suddenly everything seems safe and normal again. A backyard barbecue in Iowa seems about as far away from Greek drama as you can get. Then it happens. I reach over and pat Clem's hand, friendly and relaxed, and I feel this charge of pure electricity shoot up my arm so strong it nearly knocks me off my chair. I jerk my hand away. There's heat rising between my legs. I am afraid to look across the table at him. I start fanning myself with my paper napkin. Out of the corner of my eye, I can see Greta giving me a funny look. Charlie is still going on about Chicken McNuggets.

"Time for dessert," I say, and leap up from the table, overturning my chair.

Clem reaches over and rights it as he follows me into the kitchen, carrying a stack of dishes.

When I open the screen door to the kitchen, Nicole is bawling upstairs, as if she senses her nice little world is hanging in the balance. I climb the stairs to her room and lean over her crib, kissing her soft naked tummy. I murmur sweet nothings to soothe her as I tug her wet diaper out from under her.

I hear footsteps on the stairs and can sense someone standing at the doorway. I don't even have to turn around: I know it's Clem. I focus all my energy on wiping Nicole's bottom and the tiny crack between her legs, trying to think what I am going to say, what I am going to do to outwit fate. When I straighten up and turn around finally, holding Nicole to my breast like a shield, it is Charlie standing there in the dusky hallway, alone, smiling at us. Whatever I was going to say flies right out of my mind as if it were never there.

"They had to go," he says. "They're leaving for Florida tomorrow early, and they didn't realize how late it was getting to be."

"Florida?" I say blankly.

"Her folks have a condo down there on the beach, and they're driving down to meet them."

"Sounds serious," I say. I feel a pain I can't place and then realize that Nicole is pulling on my hair. I tug the strand of hair out from between her clenched fists.

"Clem said to tell you good-bye and thanks for supper."

I nod and hand the baby over to Charlie.

The dishes are stacked neatly in the sink where Clem must have left them. It's almost dark in the kitchen, restful. I don't bother to turn on the light. As I plunge my hands into the hot white froth, I picture Clem and Greta running in and out of the surf, framed by palm trees, and I wonder if fate ever just loses its way, like a package delivered to the wrong address. It would seem only natural. Nothing's perfect. And from a distance, we do look alike—she and I. As I am fishing in the warm water for loose knives and forks, the phone rings and I stretch out a soapy hand to answer it.

"Hi," Janelle says. "It's me."

"Don't tell me," I say. "Richard's back."

"How'd *you* know?" she says, disappointed that I jumped the gun.

"I'm psychic," I say. "So how is it this time?"

As I listen to the familiar, doomed details of their romance, I sink into a kitchen chair and close my eyes. After a minute even sitting in a chair seems to require too much effort. I slide off the chair onto the cool floor, murmuring an occasional "uh-huh." I lie on my back on the fake-brick linoleum and rest the receiver on top of both my eyelids, like one of those small plastic eye-protectors people wear under sunlamps. I pretend I am lying on the beach in Florida. Janelle's voice sounds distant and hollow, like there is an ocean between us. In Florida, the sun is blazing, I am wearing a black bikini, my scar is gone, and everything is perfect.

Monogamy

It was just like in the movies—a deathbed summons. The phone rings while my wife and I are clearing away the supper dishes and it is some stranger, a woman, calling to inform me that my father is dying and would like to see me before he goes. The phrase "before he goes" strikes me as oddly casual, as if he were just taking off for a long weekend. I don't know, I tell the woman, I'll have to think about it and call you back. She gives me the phone number in New Mexico and hangs up without any attempt to persuade or pressure me, her message simply and clearly delivered.

Now, three days later, my wife and I are driving from the Albuquerque airport to Rancho de Taos in a rented Ford Taurus to visit my dying father, whom I have not seen since 1954, when I was five years old. Flying from LA to New Mexico is like walking out of a crowded, smoky bar into Yosemite, and we're both feeling a little giddy and light-headed. The landscape seems spookily clear, like a super-realist painting.

"I feel stoned," I say, punching the radio buttons. "The altitude."

"You nervous?"

I shake my head, but Laurel reaches over and flicks my hand away from the radio. "Pick a station or else turn it off. You're giving me a headache."

"Sorry," I shrug. "Maybe I'm a little edgy."

"Well, I guess you're entitled." She slides her hand over and rests it reassuringly on my thigh. I pat her hand. Unlike my first wife, Laurel has a motherly streak.

Just past the turnoff for Los Alamos, she says, "Do you remember what he looks like?"

"Only from the pictures."

"He's old and sick now. You probably wouldn't recognize him anyway."

"I'm glad you're here," I say. "I couldn't do this without you. I would have just said forget it."

"You would not." She smiles fondly at this foolishness, which I know to be the absolute, honest truth.

We have been married two years, and she still persists in her illusions regarding my superior intelligence, virility, and worthiness. I spent my first marriage protesting that I was not really all that bad, and I seem to be spending my second protesting that I am not really all that good. For a moment I feel almost cheerful about this trip as it occurs to me how terribly cheated Mara, my first wife, will feel when she gets my message on her answer-phone explaining why I will not be able to pick up Sara and Joel as usual this Saturday. She has always wanted to meet my father, the bigamist.

It all happened when I was five. The other wife somehow stumbled upon the bitter truth and called my mother, who subsequently took an overdose of sleeping pills while I was at a neighbor kid's birthday party. I came home from the party to find my Aunt Liz crying and waiting for me. My mother had arranged for her sister to pick her up to go shopping so that there would be no chance of my coming home to find the body and being thus warped for life. I remember returning home triumphant—I had won a prize, an Etch-A-Sketch, for pinning the tail on the donkey, and somehow the game got all mixed up in my mind with my mother's death; I felt some sort of confused primal guilt—some unconscious throwback to voodoo magic—as if by sticking pins in the donkey I had unknowingly wounded my mother.

My mother's sister and husband took me in as one of their own. I called them Mom and Pop (as opposed to Mommy and Daddy, which is what I'd called my real parents). It was a large, happy, chaotic household. Six kids. Catholic. During the Kennedy era, we referred to our house as Hickory Hill and played touch football on the lawn. For the first few days and weeks, they told me my father was away on business. Since he'd always spent so much time away on business, I suppose I didn't think much of it. I was only five, with a kid's short attention span and loyalties. An only child, I imagine I was thrilled to be thrust suddenly into such a beehive of sibling activity. After a while I more or less forgot about my real father, and by the time I was old enough to remember him again, to wonder about him, I really didn't much care. I wanted to think of Mom and Pop as my real parents and my cousins as my real brothers and sisters.

When I was in third grade, Mom and Pop sat me down and told me they had legally adopted me and my name from now on was John McGuire instead of John Collins. Mom said she'd talked to my principal and teachers and they were changing all my official records. Pop said he thought it was time they told me the whole story before I heard it someplace else. He explained that my mother had taken her life because she'd found out that my father had committed bigamy. That meant he had a whole other family out west, in San Francisco—another house, another wife, another son—and that was against the law. I asked if he were in jail and Pop said no, he wasn't; after my mother died, they'd thought it best to let the whole thing drop as long as my father promised to stay away. Then I asked whether he had another car out west, another blue Buick. Pop looked surprised and said he really didn't know. There was an awkward pause, and then he asked me if I thought I understood and I said yes. Did I have any other questions? And I said no. I remember going back outside to ride my bike and suddenly thinking of another question. I ran back inside the house. "Who's older?" I hollered. "The other kid or me?" I breathed a big sigh of relief when Pop said I was older, the other little boy was only four or five. That night, lying in bed I thought about "bigmy." I'd seen some show on TV about pygmies and somehow the two fused themselves in my mind. I imagined my father had this other family of tiny dark people out there in San Francisco. It didn't really bother me as long as I was bigger.

"This is it." Laurel suddenly points to the left. "The directions say turn left at Coyote Pottery."

I hang a left, tires kicking up a storm of dusty gravel. "Does she say how far?"

"Two miles or so." Laurel puts down the map and takes a good look at the mountains, the blue sky, the painterly light. "God it's gorgeous."

"Considerate of the old fart to die in such a scenic spot," I say.

She gives me a sharp look teetering on the verge of rebuke and then smiles understandingly. "You always joke when you're anxious."

"I don't know where you get this idea I'm such a nice guy. Just don't expect too much from me here." I swerve sharply to avoid hitting a couple old mongrels sunning themselves in the bend of the road. "This isn't the movies. We're not going to fall misty-eyed into each other's arms. It's a miracle I'm even here."

She sighs and hunts around in her bag for her lipstick, then pulls down the visor and colors her lips in the small mirror.

"I wonder how much these adobes go for," I say, switching to a more neutral topic.

She pulls out a hairbrush and brushes her thick wheaty hair. "Probably a bundle. They have that funky chic look. Kind of like Mara."

I laugh. She's right on the money there.

"We'll have to buy something really nice for Sara and Joel," she says. "To make up for missing Saturday. Maybe some beaded moccasins. Or do you think that's too feminine for Joel? I mean he could care less about clothes and all." She frowns and bites her lip, trying to envision the perfect gift for my seven-year-old son.

My heart sinks a little as I reach over and squeeze her hand, knowing how much she wants a baby of her own and how much I don't. "A tomahawk would probably be more to his taste."

"That must be it up there." She strains forward in her seat. "It says to look for a pink mailbox at the end of the driveway."

I slow down to a crawl. There's still time to turn around, I think, but Laurel is already waving and smiling at someone.

My father, doped up on painkillers, sleeps all afternoon. "Pain management," they call it, Violet informs us. Upon our arrival, Violet and her sister Rose bring a pitcher of sun tea out onto the back patio and we sit there gazing at the spectacular mountain vista while Violet and Rose take turns filling us in on the gruesome history of my father's lung cancer. As they talk, a picture of my father suddenly flashes into my mind: we're in the blue Buick. He and my mother are in the front seat and I'm sitting between them. My father says, "Hit it, Johnny." I punch in the cigarette lighter and keep my eyes glued on it, ready to pounce the instant it pops back out. Then, self-importantly, I hold its glowing coils up to my father, who bends his neck down, a Camel stuck between his lips, and delicately touches the tip of the cigarette to the coils until it puffs smoke, at which point I insert the lighter back into its hole.

"You may be wondering," Rose says. "Your father and I met in Mexico—at an alternative cancer clinic, Casa Esperanza. Maybe you've heard of it?"

Laurel and I shake our heads.

Violet snorts. "Casa Rip-off."

"I was there with my husband." Rose sighs and takes a delicate sip of tea, ignoring her sister. "He passed away three years ago. When your father's sympathy card arrived, inviting me for a visit, I thought why not? There was nothing holding me in Kansas City, what with Bud gone. I don't like to fly, so I asked Violet to come along for the ride. We've been here ever since."

"It's just a matter of time now," Violet interjects bleakly.

"We talked it over and Ray, your father, insisted he'd had enough of hospitals. He wanted to come home."

"It's a hospice program," Violet says.

Rose nods enthusiastically. "These nice strangers come over

and lend you support—help with the cooking and laundry and everything, just like saints."

"I think I hear him now," Violet mumbles, disappearing inside the house.

"He had a bad morning," Rose confides in a whisper. Then she leaps up and follows Violet.

Left abruptly alone, Laurel and I exchange complicated glances. She winks as if to say, *"Coraggio!"* My heart pounds as I wait for the summons—face to face after thirty-five years—but the sisters reappear almost immediately.

"False alarm," Violet says flatly.

Rose passes around a package of Fig Newtons. Relieved at the reprieve, I take a cookie. Laurel initiates polite small talk. How do you like New Mexico? Where did you grow up? That sort of thing. Rose, the chattier one, answers all Laurel's questions, often to be haughtily contradicted on some fact by Violet. When Laurel runs out of questions, Rose says, "I imagine you noticed we're identical twins."

Startled, I take a closer look and suddenly see the resemblance even though Rose must outweigh Violet by fifty pounds; Rose's hair is starchily bouffant whereas Violet's is twisted into a messy topknot; and Rose's soft, pale complexion seems genetically unrelated to her sister's brown leathery skin.

"Of course we looked more alike when we were younger," Rose concedes.

"You mean before you blimped up," Violet needles, flapping her colorful serape and jangling her armload of silver bracelets.

Rose picks a spot of lint off her more conventional polyester slacks and ignores the jibe. "We did TV commercials. Back then they were always looking for good-looking twins." She bursts into a little jingle: "Double your pleasure, double your fun, with Doublemint, Doublemint, Doublemint gum!"

Violet shakes her head and groans. "That's enough, Rose. You'll wake up Ray."

Which is the last thing I want. Even though I've come all this way, I keep hoping he'll sleep forever.

"And what is it you do?" Violet asks me suddenly, shifting the beam of attention from Rose to me.

"I'm a box engineer." I sketch a square in air. "I design boxes for various products—mostly produce. Spinach, pineapples, alfalfa sprouts." This creates an awkward little lull in the conversation. "Laurel's a florist," I add.

"Oh really," Rose brightens. "We just love flowers."

Laurel smiles, looking around the dusty yard with not so much as a dandelion in sight. I look at my watch. Five o'clock. "Maybe we should head on over to our motel and come back in the morning."

"Oh no. He's bound to wake up soon," Rose says. "Stay for dinner. I've made a flan and some—"

"They're probably tired," Violet interrupts. "He's more alert in the mornings. Around eight or so."

We get directions to our motel in Taos proper and promise to be back bright and early. Rose looks a little crestfallen as we back out of the driveway.

At dinner that night at Doc Martin's Restaurant, recommended by *Fodor's Guide to New Mexico*, Laurel and I speculate as to my father's relationship with the sisters, who we estimate to be somewhere in their midfifties, about ten years younger than my father.

Laurel dips her sopapilla in honey and takes a bite. "There were three bedrooms," she says after she's swallowed. "Maybe they're all just friends."

"Beats me." I gesture at the waiter for another Tecate. "Come to think of it, I don't even know what my father's done for a living all these years."

"What did he do before?" she asks casually. In the past I've changed the subject whenever she's asked about my real father, and I can tell she's afraid any minute I'll start talking about the weather.

"He sold souvenirs to all the hotels in and around Philadelphia—Liberty Bell charm bracelets and swizzle sticks and pencil sharpeners, that sort of thing. Some little factory out in San Francisco manufactured them for him, which is why he was always flying out there. Supposedly."

Laurel nods and waits for me to go on. I can't think of anything else to say, and she doesn't press—another way in which she is different from my first wife. Mara was a bloodhound. Any subject you didn't want to talk about, that's what she wanted to hear about. It was no surprise when she dropped out of law school to become a psychoanalyst. To Mara, a lover was above all else a repository of deep, buried secrets; a relationship was an archaeological dig. Lying in bed, during the quiet, spent aftermath of lovemaking, she went to work. Dig. Dig. Dig. Then once she'd excavated all your broken shards and maimed statuettes, she moved on to the next guy.

The waiter brings the bill. As I sign the credit slip, I look over at Laurel and say, "I'm glad I married you. Are you glad you married me?"

She smiles and says, "I've done things I regretted more."

We get up and leave. The evening is pleasantly warm, the light just fading behind the mountains as we stroll around the plaza, looking in the shop windows at the profusion of Indian jewelry, pottery, paintings, and T-shirts. At one shop Laurel buys some tiny turquoise-and-coral posts for my daughter, Sara, who's just recently had her ears pierced, and a string tie—a sterling silver holster with a detachable six-shooter— for Joel. It is blatantly overpriced, and I don't think Joel would be caught dead wearing it. But she is so enthusiastic I don't have the heart to say anything—even though I am almost certain that Mara will end up appropriating it for herself.

When I wake up the next morning, in our unfamiliar hotel room, I know I have been dreaming about my father. Normally I do not remember my dreams, and even as I realize I have been dreaming about him, the dream itself gets away from me, like a kite I have inattentively let go of. As I try to grab hold of it, I can see the bright shape and colors drifting farther and farther away. Mara always pestered me to tell her my dreams first thing in the morning, over breakfast, and when I steadfastly maintained my nocturnal amnesia, she gloomily predicted some day I would crack up: my subconscious, so long bottled up, would suddenly erupt like Mt. St. Helens. But it was Mara, with her volumes of dream journals, who ended up going off the deep end the year after our divorce and had to be put on antidepressants for six months, while I continued to wake up reasonably sane and cheerful every morning.

"I dreamed about my father," I tell Laurel when she emerges naked and dewy from the shower.

Rummaging through her suitcase, she says, "What did you dream?"

"I can't remember the details."

"Damn. I forgot the belt to this dress." She throws the dress aside and pulls out a khaki jumpsuit instead. For a moment I am miffed at her lack of interest in my dream life, and then I remind myself that that was one of the reasons I married her.

I haul myself out of bed, walk over and yank the drapes open. "Christ, will you look at that view? I feel like I'm in Shangri-la."

She frowns at her watch. "You better shower, honey. We promised we'd be there at eight."

"Let's go sight-seeing instead," I say. "It's such a perfect day! We could drive out to the pueblo, have a picnic."

She laughs airily, as if I've made some sort of witticism, and throws me a towel.

"Looks like someone else is here," Laurel says as we pull up out in front. The house itself is surrounded by a high adobe wall, a fortified hacienda. Except for the big white satellite dish in the far corner of the yard.

The minute I take a good look at the mud-spattered van with the Florida plates and the handicapped insignia, my blood freezes. Some part of the dream floats back to me: my half-brother Jack and me, riding somewhere in the blue Buick with my father. It is summer, but we are dressed exactly alike in cheesy Halloween costumes from Woolworth's, the kind that tie in the back. Our mothers sit in the back seat dressed in bride outfits. On the radio Tony Bennett is singing "I Left My Heart in San Francisco."

My foot presses the accelerator of the rented Ford Taurus and we shoot past the house, nearly hitting a stray dog.

"What are you doing?" Laurel says.

I keep driving.

"What *are* you *doing*?" she repeats.

I pull off to the side of the road. A cloud of dust sifts over us.

"What's the matter, John?" she asks more gently.

I'm trembling, shaking my head. She slides over and wraps her arms around me, makes comforting sounds.

"I don't want to go in there." My voice sounds thin and whiny, like my seven-year-old son's. "I've *got* a family and he's not part of it. I've got Mom and Pop, I've got brothers and sisters, I've got you and Sara and Joel. I don't need him. He's nobody to me. Why do I have to see him? Just because he asks?"

"Well," Laurel says and then pauses. "It's up to you."

"For all I know, it's all Violet's big idea. He doesn't know a thing about it." I wait for her to say something.

"It's up to you," she repeats.

"Okay then. I'm not going in there." I jerk the car into gear and swirl it around, whipping up more dust. "We'll drive out to the pueblo, have a nice lunch somewhere, and then head back for Albuquerque. Okay?"

"Whatever you say." She looks straight ahead and sighs.

I hit the brakes, jolting us. "You think I'm doing the wrong thing?" I ask belligerently.

She shrugs.

"Just say what you think!"

"I just think maybe you'll regret it. That's all."

"Why? Why should I?" I pound the steering wheel with my fist. "Give me one good reason."

"I don't know. That's just how life is."

"Great!" I snort. "That's just how life is," I mutter sarcastically. But I am already slowing down, pulling in behind the muddy van.

Rose flutters out to meet us wearing a butterfly-print sundress, her pale breasts rising like dough from the scooped-out neckline. In her serape and moccasins, Violet steals up behind her, silent and surefooted as a tracker.

"He's up and waiting for you," Rose smiles gaily. "And there's someone else—" she hesitates coyly as if waiting for me to guess who.

"Your half-brother," Violet announces. "From Gainesville."

Laurel lets out a gasp, which she covers with a little cough. I've never told her about my father's other son, the pygmy. Once, in a careless postcoital moment, I'd let Mara dig it out of me, and the next thing I knew we were on our way to San Francisco to find him. This was 1967, the summer of love. Mara and I drove out from Swarthmore, where we were both sophomores, to Berkeley, where an old boyfriend of hers was in school. We tracked down my father's other wife living in a small tract house in Richmond, a few miles north of Berkeley but another world altogether. The woman was caught off guard when I (actually Mara) knocked on her door and explained who I was, but she said she'd always expected to hear from me someday. We went inside and she poured us some Tab. She was small and blond and delicate, just like my mother—only much older now of course, and faded. I was surprised. It seemed if you were going to bother with bigamy you'd want opposite types, chocolate and vanilla, not just two of the same. The woman—her name was Helen Phelps—smiled shyly and sorrowfully at me as I sat there like a bump on a log, struck dumb, while Mara interviewed her.

The basic facts were that she'd sent my father packing as soon as she found out about us. Refused to see him or even talk to him on the phone. A year later she married a widower with three small daughters. Her new husband and her son, Jack, my father's son, never got along. Last year, when Jack was sixteen, he'd run away from home, and she didn't know where he was. She'd received one postcard postmarked San Diego letting her know he was alive. Tears spilled over, and she dabbed at her eyes with a crumpled Kleenex. Then she asked about me, and Mara recited an exaggerated résumé of all my athletic and scholastic achievements—from Little League pitcher to National Merit winner (actually I was only a finalist). Helen smiled, looking genuinely pleased and impressed. When Mara trailed off, Helen patted my hand and said, "You don't know how relieved I am. I always felt so guilty, even though I hadn't known, of course. Especially when I heard about what your mother did to herself. I was always afraid I'd ruined your life, that you'd grow up to be some sort of addict or criminal. But look at you."

At that point she got up and walked over to the buffet in the dining area and pulled out a picture album. She poured us each more Tab as we flipped through the pages—mostly snapshots of the three girls—but every once in a while there'd be a picture of Jack—on a tricycle, a skateboard, a Suzuki, hunched over the handlebars, always about to take off. I didn't want to look at him, but I couldn't help myself. He wasn't dark and he wasn't little. In fact, as Mara pointed out, he looked a lot like me. I shot her a dirty look and an awkward silence ensued. Tactfully, Helen said she guessed that was all and closed the cover, but Mara—dig, dig—reached out and flipped open the album to the first couple of pages, which Helen had skipped. My father holding the infant as if it were a prize-winning trout. My father, Helen, and little Jack on a cable car. Little Jack and my father standing in front of a Chinese restaurant, holding chopsticks to their heads like Martian antennae. I excused myself and went to the bathroom. I sat down on the pink-shag toilet-seat cover and held my head in my hands. With my eyes closed, all I could see was the blown-up snapshot my mother always kept on the mantel of our house: my father and me, grinning like idiots, holding Liberty Bell swizzle sticks to our heads like Martian antennae. If he had to have another kid, why couldn't he at least have had a daughter? I practiced some deep breathing, splashed cold water on my face, and walked casually back out, to the living room.

When we left, Mara and I had a huge fight. A real knock-down-drag-out. I stayed in Berkeley, entranced by all the sunshine and love beads, while Mara returned to Pennsylvania. But a year later she transferred to Cal, and we shared a room in a ramshackle house on Woolsey Street. Even though (as far as I knew) she lived twenty minutes away, I never saw Helen again or heard from her, except for once about three years later. I received a short note postmarked Gainesville, Florida, and forwarded from Swarthmore, informing me that Jack was missing in action in Vietnam. She said she thought I'd like to know.

"Why didn't you mention he was coming?" I say to Violet as I follow her out of the bright sunlight inside the cool, dark adobe, trying to sound offhand and pleasant. "I'm not much for surprises."

"Well," Rose smiles beseechingly and wrings her hands together, "we really weren't sure he'd be here—"she lowers her voice to a confidential whisper—"we didn't really know if he traveled much, you know, in his condition."

"Your father thought you might not come if you knew," Violet says, never one to mince words.

"What condition is that?" I ask, wanting to prepare myself, not wanting my facial expression to betray any shock or disgust, but she is already sliding open the screen door to the patio and yoo-hooing our arrival.

Laurel grabs my hand from behind and squeezes hard—half-reprimand, half-encouragement. I squeeze back—half-apology, half-SOS.

The bright sun blinds me for a moment, and all I see is the

glint of metal, a pair of those crutches you fit your wrists through, not the kind you tuck under your armpits when you break your leg skiing. My first thought is relief—at least he *has* arms and legs. Rose does the introductions. Jack and his wife, Anita, are sitting in lawn chairs drinking sun tea. We all shake hands. Laurel sits in the one remaining chair while I stand awkwardly, waiting for Rose to drag out more chairs. When I offer to help, she shoos me back outside. From the waist up, Jack is massive and muscular. His tanned arms seem to wrestle the flimsy sleeves of his Hawaiian shirt, while his legs lie defeated inside the baggy jeans. He reminds me of one of those fabulous hybrid beasts in my daughter's mythological coloring book. While Jack and I silently sniff each other like hostile dogs—you can practically hear the low growls in the back of our throats—our wives start to chat amiably about this and that, nervously glancing over at the two of us every few seconds, as if afraid one of us will suddenly sink his teeth into the other's flesh and they will have to leap up and drag us apart before the fur starts flying. Jack lights up a Camel. Rose slides the door open and drags a folding chair along the patio. The screech of metal against the concrete makes me shiver.

"He's awake," Violet suddenly looms in the doorway and makes her announcement. I'm so generally distracted that for an instant I almost say "Who?" and then I remember she means him—our father.

"Have you seen him yet?" I ask Jack.

He shakes his head. "We just got here 'bout ten minutes before you all. Took turns, drove straight through."

I take this as a sort of reproach of Laurel's and my softness and extravagance, flying that relatively short distance and then spending the night in a fancy hotel. Jack stubs out his cigarette, hoists himself up, and steadies himself on his crutches, weight forward on those sumo-wrestler arms. As I follow along behind him, I notice that he has an artificial foot, the left one. Then it occurs to me that he may have seen him, our father, before this. He may have been in touch with him all along. The thought is a disquieting one for some reason, and I shove it aside. As I pass by Laurel, she shakes her head as if to say, *Jesus, this is all too weird*, and gives me a discreet thumbs-up sign. It seems like a long, silent walk through the cavernous living room and down the hall toward the bedroom. To break the tension I ask, "How's your mother doing?"

"Better than us," Jack says. "She's dead. Year ago Christmas."

"I'm sorry. She seemed like a nice woman."

"She was okay." He shrugs inside his crutches. "Too bad she kept marrying such dickheads."

"If you feel like that, then why'd you come?" I say, a bit stiffly. My tone surprises me since I feel pretty much the same way myself.

He comes to a halt, as if taking a rest, and looks around. Violet and Rose are already waiting in the bedroom. "Let's cut the bullshit," Jack whispers. "The old guy's loaded. He started some Philadelphia Cheese-steak dive out on the highway, and twenty years later Taco Bell comes along and buys him out." He takes a look at my face and shakes his head. "You didn't know? For real?"

"How would I know? We haven't been in touch for thirty-five years. Have you?"

"Not face to face. Every once in a while, when I was in a jam, I'd drop him a line and he'd send me a few bucks." Jack starts down the hall again. "He might be a dickhead, but at least he's not a stingy dickhead like the second one she married. That guy was pathological."

Rose tiptoes to the bedroom door and motions us in. A rented hospital bed with metal bars is positioned center stage underneath the window, and he is propped up on pillows, wearing some natty navy pajamas with white piping, the creases still visible, as if the sisters have just taken them out of the package for our arrival. The sun shining through the window above his head creates a fuzzy halo effect, and it is not until I circle around to the side of the bed that I get a good look at him. Immediately I feel all choked up. I suppose I expected him to look like some weathered version of his younger self, an antique Tab Hunter, but he looks more like Gandhi after his last hunger strike. Jack and I stand on either side of the bed, like silent bookends, and when our eyes meet I can see he is as shaken as I am. Our outlaw father has always seemed larger than life, and now suddenly, lying there fondling the remote-control device, he seems smaller than life. I feel cheated.

"John, Jack," he rasps. "Good of you to come." In his nervousness he accidentally blips on the TV, which shouts to life, an old Dick Van Dyke rerun. Black and white. For a moment I am back in our living room in King of Prussia, lying on a pillow on the beige plush carpet, the screen wavering as my mother runs the vacuum cleaner overhead. Jack lowers himself into a chair, starts to light up a Camel, and then thinks better of it. I drag a chair over to my side of the bed, and the three of us sit there watching Rob and Laura and little Robbie, the all-American family. Spellbound. My father laughs along with the laugh track, and a couple of times Jack kind of lets out a short bark. After maybe five minutes, the show ends. I reach over and hit the off button.

An awkward silence shadows the room. Jack fondles his un-lit Camel. Finally the old man clears his throat and says, "Rose and Violet get the house. The rest is yours, fifty-fifty."

"Come on now," Jack gives him a light shoulder punch. "You're not going anywhere."

"You believe in heaven and hell?"

Simultaneously Jack nods and I shake my head. He and I look at each other with something beyond curiosity: a few ejaculations sooner or later and we could have wound up being each other.

"I suppose in most people's book a bigamist goes straight to hell. Do not pass Go." The old man pauses, wincing and grimacing, as a bolt of pain seems to work its way through his body. "Most people go by the book. The letter of the law. Not the spirit." He taps a finger to his chest. A theatrical gesture.

Jack and I just stand there looking half-stricken, half-skeptical, like amateurish supporting actors. Any second I expect to hear the director yell "Cut!" Then, as if reading my mind, my father says, "You ever see that old movie *The Bigamist* with Edmond O'Brien?" We shake our heads. "Good movie," he says. His voice rattles like paper. Jack picks up the glass of water from the night table and gives him a couple of sips. The old man turns his head slightly to the left, toward me. "I don't know if you remember, you must have been about four. I was out of town, and your mother and you decided to drive down to Nana's place in Rehoboth for a few days. Coming back, you had an accident on the turnpike. Nothing too serious. Your mother had to wear a collar for a few weeks. New headlight and bumper. You were asleep in the back seat and just sprained your wrist."

I nod slowly as he speaks, and suddenly I can feel the motion of the car underneath me, the sound of the tires, soft music on the radio, the rhythmic pelt of rain on the metal roof, and then the loud, screeching crash. I'm thrown onto the floor. My mother is screaming, "Oh my God, oh my God."

"Well," my father clears his dry throat, "when Lois called me and told me—she was scared I'd be mad about the goddamn car—I shook for an hour, just sitting there alone in my hotel room imagining what could have happened. Just like that—" he tries to snap his fingers together but doesn't have the strength—"in one minute, my family could have been wiped out. I could have been all alone in the world. Nothing. I guess everyone always knows that, on some level, but right then it really hit me. Hard."

Jack's nodding his head as if he knows just what he means, and then I happen to glimpse myself in the mirror across the room and see that I am nodding right along with him. I flash on Mara's calling me from the airport, shouting to make herself heard over Sara's wailing—at that time she was a couple months pregnant with Joel—telling me about how the plane had lost an engine and had to make an emergency landing in Omaha. My hands were trembling so violently I had trouble fitting the receiver back in its cradle, and as I dined alone at a restaurant that evening, toying with my food, I kept imagining that I was a widower delaying my return to an empty house.

"I'm not making any excuses," he says, "but a couple of months later I met Helen, *your* mother—"he turns his head in Jack's direction—"and she reminded me a lot of Lois. It was like we already knew each other from somewhere—she felt it, too. She was all alone, new to the city. We had lunch a couple of times. One thing led to another. Somehow, at first, I never got around to mentioning I was married, and then it was just too late, things had gone too far." He pauses to spit some phlegm into a Kleenex. "She was pregnant. So I did the only thing I could—I married her. I told myself I'd think of something. After a while I could just say it wasn't working out and ask for a divorce. But somehow I never got around to that either. Kept putting it off. Just couldn't bring myself to let go."

"How're you boys doing?" Rose pokes her bouffant head inside the doorway. "Like any iced tea or sodas or anything?"

We shake our heads and she ducks back out.

"Then it was too late. She found out about Lois and Johnny here. And that was that. The shit really hit the fan on both ends." He sinks back into the pillows and closes his eyes. Jack and I wait, not looking at each other. Outside the window a couple of magpies swoop by. The blue mountains look like a painted backdrop. I wish Jack would get up and leave us alone because there's a question I want to ask but not with him in the room. Then just when I think maybe the old guy's nodded off, he opens his eyes and says, "I lost everyone."

I think of the sisters but don't say anything, not wanting to interrupt.

"It was my punishment for trying to hedge my bets, beat out the odds." His voice is almost gone, a gravelly whisper, but he keeps going, on a roll. He waves away the water Jack offers him. "It was like I'd got myself this spare family. Just in case. Anything happened to the one, I'd still be okay. I wouldn't be left with nothing. All alone. I always hated hotels and restaurants. Sleeping alone. Eating alone. Flirting with the waitresses so you wouldn't seem pitiful." He lapses into an exhausted silence.

Jack tamps his Camel nervously on his knee, clears his throat, and says, "Did you love both of them?"

I look up startled. That was my question. I catch Jack's eye, and in the tension of the moment something sort of eases between the two of us.

"Of course I did," our father snaps, like we're two slow-witted kids who haven't been paying attention. "Why the hell else?"

I stand up. "We better let you get some rest."

Jack nods and reaches for his crutches.

Over Rose's feeble protests to stay, the four of us—Jack, Anita, Laurel, and I—drive up the road for some lunch at La Ultima Café. We order nachos and a pitcher of beer. Our wives seem to have hit it off like long-lost sisters, talking about the joys and sorrows of being a stepmother. Jack has a teenage daughter from a previous marriage. When the beer arrives, I start pouring and hand Anita a glass, but she shakes her head and reaches for her water glass instead.

"She's pregnant," Laurel says brightly, and even though I can detect no edge to her voice, no reproach or self-pity, I flinch a little inwardly.

"Congratulations!" I toast Jack and Anita. We all clink glasses.

Sitting next to Jack, I notice that if he had the use of his legs, he would be at least two inches taller than I, well over six feet. And I feel a twinge of the old voodoo guilt, as if somehow my childhood image of him as a pygmy—in some distorted and mysterious way—managed to hit its mark. I feel like I owe him an apology of some sort but can't think what. For mopping the halls of a state psychiatric facility in Santa Rosa—C.O. duty—

while Jack was tiptoeing through the rice paddies, ducking enemy fire? For wishing he didn't exist and then forgetting he did?

"So what do you think of the old man?" Jack says, taking a deep drag on his cigarette.

I shrug. "I guess I feel sorry for him."

Laurel looks at me, nacho poised in midair, with a surprised expression, then smiles.

"Same here," Jack says. "Never thought I'd hear myself say that."

"Me neither." I pour more beer into his almost-empty glass.

"You ever get to Florida?" Jack says.

Laurel and I take the six-o'clock flight back to LA. Jack and Anita stay on, planning to do a little sight-seeing in their van before heading back east. The flight home is uneventful; I feel oddly relaxed and peaceful, as if we have just spent a week lying on the beach. The next morning, Sunday, I decide to take a quick drive over to Mara's place in Venice Beach and give the kids their New Mexico presents. When I arrive, Sara and Joel are still in their rooms getting dressed. Usually, on Saturdays, I just sit in the car and honk till the kids come out, but today Mara invites me inside, pours me a cup of coffee, eager to hear all about my father. I recognize the old flannel shirt she's wearing as one of mine, and as I sit there drinking her familiar-tasting coffee in my former kitchen, listening to my son and daughter's bickering, like distant gunfire in the bedroom, I feel right at home. I feel, suddenly, like a bigamist. I can see myself puttering through my Sunday chores—mowing the scruffy lawn, washing the car, dropping the kids off at a Disney matinee, and then speeding back home to laze around in bed with Mara till it's time to go pick them up again. I can feel myself lying pleasantly naked, pleasantly expectant, in a shaft of warm sunlight on the unmade bed while Mara putters in the bathroom, inserting her diaphragm. I can feel my hands slide underneath the warm flannel of her shift. Like a horse that knows the way home, my body settles into the familiar rhythm, the same old destination. But then suddenly the channel flips: I picture Laurel sitting out on our tiny patio, working the Sunday *Times* crossword puzzle, frowning and erasing with the pure concentration of a child, waiting for me to come back and tell her how much Sara and Joel loved their presents, how perfect they were, and I am suddenly anxious, almost frantic, to get back to my real wife, my real home.

"Hey, get a move on, you lazy bums!" I shout down the hall. "I'm counting. Ten, nine, eight, ..."

Sara bursts into the kitchen, followed by Joel with only one sneaker. I kneel down and open my arms and whirl them around a few times before setting them back down. Joel staggers around the kitchen shouting, "I'm drunk! I'm drunk!"

Sara straddles my knee. "Which pocket?"

I point and she fishes out a small white box. She holds her breath as she opens it. Her face breaks into a big relieved smile. "Oh boy, earrings!" She runs over to Mara. "Put them in, Mom."

"Very pretty," Mara appraises the earrings and nods at me as she tucks Sara's long hair behind her ears and hastily jabs in the tiny posts.

"Ouch!" Sara yelps indignantly and glares at her.

"Sorry," Mara shrugs.

I think how much more gentle and maternal Laurel's touch is, how slow and meticulous. Watching Sara massage her earlobe, I suddenly remember the way Mara would slap suntan lotion on my back, as if I were keeping her from something truly important. And the way Laurel smoothes it on—like an act of love.

"What about me?" Joel demands.

"C'mere, buster." I take the gun-and-holster string tie out of my pocket and lasso it around his neck.

"What is it?" he says suspiciously.

"It's a Texas string tie," I say, sounding as enthusiastic as possible.

"It's called a bolo," Mara informs us.

"Look. The gun comes out." Sara takes the little silver gun out of the holster and puts it back in.

Joel yanks the thing off over his head and drops it on the table, then runs off to show me his latest Matchbox truck. Sara disappears to the bathroom to preen in front of the mirror in her new earrings. I pick up the abandoned string tie, glad Laurel isn't here to see what a flop it is. In my mind's eye, I see her getting up from the chaise lounge, putting aside the crossword puzzle, and walking inside the silent, empty house, wondering what to do next.

"I think Laurel and I are going to have a baby," I blurt out all of a sudden, surprising myself.

Mara raises her eyebrows and lowers her coffee cup. "I thought you always said you didn't want to be one of those guys with two sets of kids. Old and new. Like golf clubs."

I shrug. "I've said a lot of dumb things in my time, as you were always quick to point out."

"Well, I suppose with your real father dying you must—"

"No free psychoanalysis," I say. "Please. It's Sunday, a day of rest."

"Well then, congratulations, I guess."

I don't bother to tell her it hasn't happened yet.

She picks up the bolo and slips it around her neck, sliding the little holster up underneath her shirt collar. I smile to myself.

"What's so funny?" she says.

"Nothing." I stand up. "I better get going. Tell the kids I'll see them Saturday." On sudden impulse, I bend over and plant a clumsy kiss on the top of her head, in the fragrant part of her dark hair, like a thin white scar. "Heigh-ho Silver." I tug the metal tip of the string tie.

She draws the tiny gun from its holster, takes aim, and pretends to shoot me. I clutch my heart and stagger out the door.

Other Iowa Short Fiction Award and
John Simmons Short Fiction Award Winners

1989
Lent: The Slow Fast,
Starkey Flythe, Jr.
Judge: Gail Godwin

1989
Line of Fall, Miles Wilson
Judge: Gail Godwin

1988
The Long White,
Sharon Dilworth
Judge: Robert Stone

1988
The Venus Tree,
Michael Pritchett
Judge: Robert Stone

1987
Fruit of the Month, Abby Frucht
Judge: Alison Lurie

1987
Star Game, Lucia Nevai
Judge: Alison Lurie

1986
Eminent Domain, Dan O'Brien
Judge: Iowa Writers' Workshop

1986
Resurrectionists, Russell Working
Judge: Tobias Wolff

1985
Dancing in the Movies,
Robert Boswell
Judge: Tim O'Brien

1984
Old Wives' Tales,
Susan M. Dodd
Judge: Frederick Busch

1983
Heart Failure, Ivy Goodman
Judge: Alice Adams

1982
Shiny Objects, Dianne Benedict
Judge: Raymond Carver

1981
The Phototropic Woman,
Annabel Thomas
Judge: Doris Grumbach

1980
Impossible Appetites,
James Fetler
Judge: Francine du Plessix Gray

1979
Fly Away Home, Mary Hedin
Judge: John Gardner

1978
A Nest of Hooks, Lon Otto
Judge: Stanley Elkin

1977
The Women in the Mirror,
Pat Carr
Judge: Leonard Michaels

1976
The Black Velvet Girl,
C. E. Poverman
Judge: Donald Barthelme

1975
Harry Belten and the
Mendelssohn Violin Concerto,
Barry Targan
Judge: George P. Garrett

1974
After the First Death There Is
No Other, Natalie L. M. Petesch
Judge: William H. Gass

1973
The Itinerary of Beggars,
H. E. Francis
Judge: John Hawkes

1972
The Burning and Other Stories,
Jack Cady
Judge: Joyce Carol Oates

1971
Old Morals, Small Continents,
Darker Times,
Philip F. O'Connor
Judge: George P. Elliott

1970
The Beach Umbrella,
Cyrus Colter
Judges: Vance Bourjaily
and Kurt Vonnegut, Jr.